OPERATOR 5:
ROCKETS FROM HELL

ROCKETS FROM HELL

By Curtis Steele

STEEGER BOOKS • 2020

PUBLISHING HISTORY

"Rockets from Hell" originally appeared in the February, 1936 (Vol. 6, No. 3) issue of
   Operator #5 magazine. Copyright © 2020 by Argosy Communications, Inc. All
   rights reserved.

CHAPTER 1
EMPIRE AT STAKE

I T WAS eleven minutes past eight in the evening when the strange sound was first heard in the skies, off the coast of Florida. It was a weird, whistling noise such as might be made by a large object traveling through the air with the speed of a shell—except that the noise was ten times louder than that made by any shell. It came from the direction of the Atlantic Ocean, whined high above the Florida Keys, then swung northward. At the time mentioned, the sound was recorded on the drum of the seismograph at the Naval Observatory at Key West. So powerful was the aerial disturbance that it caused the indicator needle of the delicate instrument to vibrate in the same manner as during a minor earth tremor.

However, the seismograph almost at once returned to normal, and the sound in the skies abruptly died away—just as the hum of a departing airplane dies out, but considerably faster....

Less than ten minutes later, the same sound was heard in the night skies above Tampa. Jacksonville and Charleston heard the noise in quick succession. Telephone calls began to pour into the offices of the Coast and Geodetic Survey in the Department of Commerce Building in Washington. Panicky queries from the cities where the sound had been heard remained unanswered, for perhaps another fifteen minutes—and then the nature, and

The night was garish with flame as wreckage
from the shipyards was hurled into the air!

destination, of the noise was partially ascertained in a horrible
and gruesome manner.

Newport News, a vital United States naval base, was the
destination of that whistling noise!

From the skies it descended, taking shape and form. But the
thing which was making the sound was traveling almost with

2

the speed of light. Men's eyes turned upward as the sound grew
louder in the passing of split seconds, filling their ears with its
horrid whistling, which was suddenly turned to a tremendous
screeching. In the second that they were vouchsafed a glimpse
of the speeding thing, they saw an object which rather resembled a huge cigar. It flashed downward toward the shipyards of

3

Newport News like a comet, giving off iridescent sparks as it cleaved through the air.

One moment it was far above them; the next, it had struck—struck full into the center of the *Granite State,* the newly completed and largest capital ship of the United States Navy, destined to be the flagship of the Atlantic Fleet.

Besides the U.S.S. *Granite State,* there were, in the dry docks of Newport News at the time the rocket struck, two more heavy cruisers in the course of construction, two light cruisers, two submarines and seven sleek destroyers. These ships were being rushed to completion in accordance with the plans of the Navy Department to build the United States Navy up to the full strength sanctioned by the Washington and London Naval Treaties.

Those plans were knocked into a cocked hat at the moment that the whistling thing from the skies struck the *Granite State.*

The explosion that followed was heard as far north as Bridgeport, Connecticut, as far west as Chattanooga, Tennessee. In Norfolk and Portsmouth, across the watery surface of Hampton Roads from Newport News, not a window was left unshattered. Buildings trembled, and the sidewalks cracked in hundreds of places. The night was made garish with flame as tall geysers of wreckage were hurtled into the air to the accompaniment of explosion after explosion.

The waters of Chesapeake Bay were cluttered with the mangled remnants of men and ships. Burning spars floated out to the ocean.

Of Newport News, no single trace remained. There were no

more dry docks, no more canteens, no more ships. The *Granite State* and her sister ships were as completely destroyed as if they had never been built. And the largest shipyard in America was wiped entirely from the face of the earth.

Four thousand men died in that cataclysm—mechanics, carpenters, marines, sailors, cooks, hangers on; as well as a contingent of two hundred and fifty midshipmen from the Naval Academy at Annapolis, who had been making an inspection of the construction operations.

The first major blow had been struck in what was to be the strangest war of annihilation ever launched against America…!

THE BOY was running fast, desperately, weaving from side to side to avoid the slugs that whined through the air all about him. His lithe young body was bent far forward at the waist, and his feet pistoned up and down as he called upon the last reserve ounces of his strength to get him away from the flaming death which pursued him. Beads of sweat oozed out on his pug-nosed, freckled face, and his matted hair fell down over his eyes. His breath was beginning to come in pained gasps, but he ran on, stumbling, recovering his balance, and forcing himself by superhuman effort.

Behind him, orange spurts of flame lanced through the night across the marshy flats of New Jersey. A bullet grazed his side, and he fell forward, headlong, in the mire. He lay there, panting, exhausted, trying to force air into his tortured lungs.

The firing behind him ceased, and dark forms raced toward him. Guttural shouts came to him across the flatlands—shouts of vindictive triumph—as his pursuers closed in.

The bullet hadn't injured the boy, but the desperate race across that mile of marshland, with hot lead whipping the air all about him, had drained him of strength.

Now he raised his head, saw his foremost pursuers only a hundred yards away. They were advancing now, grimly. Their shouts had ceased. Once they had him again....

Agonized words came from his panting lips: "Oh, God, I've got to get away from them! I've got to tell—Jimmy...!"

Ahead lay a strip of white concrete—a road. How far? With his head swimming as it was, he could not judge. But he must make it.

Desperation drove him up to his knees, to his feet. He wavered a moment, shut his eyes, opened them again, and plunged ahead, running blindly, wildly.

Behind him, hoarse shouts of anger sounded. Guns barked again. Slugs whined. He could never make that road. It was no use. He had no more strength. His feet wouldn't lift anymore. He wasn't running now, but stumbling blindly. It was a dreadful effort to drag each foot from the mire that seemed to cling to it. Slowly, he slumped to the ground again, unconscious. And the grim killers came toward him....

A LONG, low roadster hummed its chant of power as it ate up mile after mile of Jersey road. The long, white stretch of macadam ribboned between its wheels at a dizzy speed.

The young man who drove that car sat hunched over the wheel, tense, tight-lipped, eyes straight ahead, unblinking. The dancing headlights cast a wide, bright swath upon the road ahead, showing it empty of traffic, lined on either side by marshy fields. The young man kept his foot pressed on the accelerator so that it seemed to be jammed into the floorboards. The needle of the speedometer wavered at the top of the dial, close to the hundred mark. Wind whipped around the edges of the windshield, into the faces of the driver and the trim young girl who sat beside him.

The girl's chestnut hair streamed back with the wind. Her red lips were parted in anxiety, and there was an urgent desperation in her eyes.

She asked her companion, shouting so as to be heard above the wind, "Do you think we'll make it, Jimmy? God! If they should kill Tim—"

"We'll make it, Diane!" Jimmy grated. "It's somewhere along here that the fool kid said he'd meet us. There—" He took one hand from the wheel, pointed across the fields at dark, running figures, spreading out fan-wise behind a single, forlorn shape that stumbled blindly forward. Flashes of fire lanced through the night toward that running figure.

The chestnut-haired girl clutched the side of the roadster with a hand whose knuckles were white with strain. "Jimmy!" she cried. "That's Tim. God! They're after him. He's wounded. They'll kill him!"

The driver's lips twisted into a thin, grim line. Muscles ridged along his jawbone as he yanked his foot from the accelerator, clamped it down on the brake pedal. Powerful hydraulic brakes caused the tires to screech as the long car skidded around in the road, screamed to a stop at right angles to its former position.

The headlights now splayed out over the marsh field, limned the figure of the boy, crumpled on the ground, with sinister, dark shapes creeping up on him.

Before the roadster had come to a complete stop, Jimmy had let go of the wheel. He was bending over, his slim, nimble fingers working swiftly at a long box screwed into the floorboard at his feet. The lid of the box came up. Out of that box came a deadly Thompson submachine gun, which Jimmy thrust into the girl's hands. "Cover me, Diane!" he ordered tightly. "I'm going after Tim!"

Diane took the clumsy weapon, nodded eagerly, and arose in her seat, resting the barrel on the top of the windshield. Her lips were moving in silent prayer as Jimmy leaped over the side of the car, raced across the field toward the unconscious form of the boy, Tim, and toward the dark silent men who moved toward the lad. In his hand had appeared the automatic which he had snatched from a shoulder holster. He ran lightly, swiftly, the gun held in front of him. He did not deign to crouch, to weave, as the dark shapes out on the field suddenly turned their weapons on him, and orange flame spurted toward him from a dozen guns.

Behind him, the girl, Diane, was saying, "Oh, God, save them both. Spare them, oh, God!"

Even as her lips moved, she pressed the trip of the submachine gun, sent a spurt of lead past Jimmy, toward the dark figures beyond him.

She had shot high, and she hit none of them. They continued to advance, still shooting, and Jimmy sprayed slugs from his automatic in their direction as he ran. He emptied his gun, flipped out the clip and replaced it with a fresh one without shortening his pace.

IN A moment he was close to the slumped figure of the boy. He bent beside him, his eyes filled with anxiety. "Tim!" he exclaimed. "Timmy boy! Are you hurt? It's Jimmy!"

The boy did not stir.

Jimmy put a hand on him, repeated in agonized voice: "Tim! It's Jimmy Christopher! Tim! Do you hear me?"

The boy stirred, raised his head. In the dark he smiled weakly. "Jimmy! I—knew you'd come!"

"Thank God!" Jimmy Christopher exclaimed. He heard the machine gun in the roadster stuttering behind him, raised his head and saw that the dark shapes of the attackers were close now. Several of them were down, hit by machine-gun slugs. But there were many who were unhurt, whom Diane had not been able to reach with her weapon, because Jimmy and Tim were in the line of fire.

These were racing forward now, firing as they came. Lead whistled about them. A bullet tugged at Jimmy's arm, another splashed up mud not an inch from Tim's head.

The boy, Tim, thrust a small leather notebook into Jimmy Christopher's hand. "That's their book of plans, Jimmy. I—got it. Take it and run. I—can't make it. I've got—no breath left."

Jimmy Christopher took the little book, dropped it into his pocket.

Jimmy Christopher sent leaden death into the ranks of the pursuers!

"Hell, kid! You really think I'd go?" He raised his head and laughed defiantly above the chatter of the machine gun—above the sound of the short, vicious explosions from the guns in the hands of the advancing attackers.

He got to his feet, a tall, slim, lithe figure, outlined mercilessly in the glare of the headlights of the car behind him on the road. He took a single step forward, which put him spraddle-legged above the boy.

And then, like some young, fearless war-god of ages past, he stood there and traded shots with those advancing shapes. Their guns spouted lead, and it whistled about him, whining shrilly. His own automatic barked swiftly nine times, and each time he shot, one of those shapes toppled to the mud. His aim, uncannily unerring, stopped the rush for one short second.

But there were too many of those dark shapes, and they didn't stop for long. In an instant, a hoarse, guttural voice among them shouted some words in a foreign tongue, and once more the rush commenced.

But that moment of respite had been enough for Jimmy Christopher. He slid his empty gun into its holster, stooped swiftly, and swung the limp boy to his shoulder, turned and ran, zigzagging now, toward the road and the car.

Shouts of rage sounded behind them, and more shots came. The machine gun had ceased firing, for now Jimmy Christopher and his burden were directly in front of the car.

The pursuers gained each moment. Jimmy half-turned, saw that they were closing in on him, and suddenly dropped to one knee in the mud.

As if she had been waiting for that very action, the girl in the car let loose with the machine gun. The hail of lead screamed over his head, mowed through the pursuers like a huge scythe. Back and forth across their line she fanned the Thompson, then suddenly ceased.

And instantly, Jimmy Christopher was up, running hard. Burdened as he was, he made the last fifty yards in an incredibly swift sprint, ducked around to the side of the car, out of the glare of the headlights, and dumped the boy into the open rumble seat.

He swung back to the side door, reached up and took the machine gun from Diane's hands.

"Get behind the wheel!" he panted. "We've got to get away!" HE KNELT on one knee beside the car, sent the whipping lead from the hot gun into the on-swarming ranks of the pursuers. Dozens had already been killed. He dropped a dozen more.

Yet they seemed to come in increasing numbers, not caring whether they died or not. It was uncanny. Sweat stood out on Jimmy Christopher's brow as he held his finger on the trip and sent leaden death hurtling across the field.

The girl backed the car around, and Jimmy leaped to the running board, fired a last burst before the roadster roared into dizzy speed, tearing through the night back along the way it had come.

Behind them, many shapes swept onto the white road. Shot after shot crashed after the fleeing car. But the bulletproof metal of the powerful, Diesel-engine roadster turned the slugs away.

In a matter of seconds, the car had swung out of sight around a curve.

Another half-mile Diane sped before she began to abate the giddy pace. And then, ahead of them, there appeared a group of headlights, approaching swiftly.

Jimmy Christopher, who had thrown the machine gun into the car and was clinging to the windshield, called out, "Slow up, Diane. That must be the state troopers."

The approaching cars, three in number, swept up abreast of them, and their headlights bathed the roadster in light. Jimmy Christopher waved to them to stop, leaped off the running board and ran toward the uniformed man who descended.

This man was heavy-set and square-jawed. His sleeve carried the insignia of a sergeant of State Police. He frowned at Jimmy, demanding, "You the guy that phoned the barracks?"

Jimmy Christopher nodded. "You took plenty of time getting here!" He gestured toward the road behind. "You'll find a slew of dead men out there, a little way back—and if you're quick, you'll find a lot of 'em alive and kicking. The boy I told you about is safe. He's right there in the rumble seat. Hurry, Sergeant, if you want to catch any of them. They'll be getting out of there fast now."

"Just a minute!" the sergeant interrupted, as half a dozen of his men crowded around them. "What's this all about? I brought three squads out on the strength of your goofy phone call. Now you come dashing up here and tell me there's something of an army out on the flatlands. What is this—a fairy story? This is Jersey; it ain't Ethiopia. We don't have—"

Jimmy broke in hurriedly. "I told you on the phone, Sergeant, that there was a headquarters of foreign espionage agents out there, and that's all I'm at liberty to tell you now. You've got to act quickly if you are going to catch any of them. Here—"

He extracted from his pocket a flat silver case, which he snapped open with a motion of his thumbnail. Within it was a sheet of paper under a mica cover, which he extended for the sergeant to read. It read:

THE WHITE HOUSE
Washington

To Whom It May Concern:

The identity of the bearer of this letter must be kept strictly confidential.

He is Operator 5 of the United States Intelligence Service.

The signature at the bottom of that letter was that of the President of the United States of America.*

---

* AUTHOR'S NOTE: Readers of the previous chronicles of the exploits of Operator 5 will already have recognized in Jimmy Christopher the young man who is the ace operative of the United States Secret Service, known to his friends as Jimmy Christopher, and in the records of the Intelligence Service only as Operator 5. They will also have recognized as old friends, Diane Elliot and Tim Donovan—Diane, the star newspaper reporter for the Amalgamated Press, who has often risked her life in the past in assisting Jimmy Christopher; and Tim Donovan, the freckle-faced Irish lad whom Operator 5 met one night on the East Side of New York, and whom he virtually adopted as a younger brother. Tim is too young to qualify as a

THE STATE Police sergeant read that strange note twice, then glanced suspiciously at Jimmy. "If you're Operator 5," he barked, "I'm the King of Denmark! I've heard of that guy. You don't look—"

He stopped as the girl from the roadster came hurrying up to them, accompanied by the boy, Tim, who was a little pale and still breathing hard, but otherwise unhurt.

Diane exclaimed, "Please, Sergeant, you must believe us! You're wasting valuable time. I can vouch to you that this is really Operator 5. This lad is Tim Donovan. He just escaped from those men back there, after a gunfight." Diane swung upon the State Trooper the battery of her vivid, blue eyes. "You look to me like a quick-thinking, brave man. I know you won't hesitate to go after those murderers and bring them to justice. The whole nation will join in your praise, Sergeant!"

The trooper softened under her glance, threw his shoulders back and his chest out. "We'll get 'em, Miss—though I don't know what it's all about. I never heard of such a thing. We heard the firing a couple of miles back. It sounded like a machine gun. Who are those guys, anyway?"

regular Secret Service operative. He therefore acts as Jimmy's assistant in an unofficial capacity until such time as he reaches the proper age to qualify. Tim's association with Jimmy Christopher has taught him many things that the average boy of his age is generally totally unaware of, and, as readers of previous stories will recall, he has often been the instrument of saving Jimmy Christopher's life when Operator 5 had nothing to rely upon but the Irish lad's nimble wit.

15

Jimmy Christopher sighed. "They are the agents of some foreign power, Sergeant, the identity of which we have not yet been able to discover. They have been plotting some major move against the United States. By this time they're all gone anyway, and I doubt if it'll do any good to follow them."

Tim Donovan broke in. "But you can raid their headquarters, anyway. I just got away from there. It's in an old racing stable straight across the field—"

"I know the place," the sergeant said suddenly. "I been wondering what's been going on around there for the last few weeks. Lots of guys going and coming. They said they were starting a P.W.A. project, and I never bothered to check up. There's so many of them P.W.A.—"

"Look here, Sergeant," Jimmy interrupted him, "if you're going to do anything about it, now is the time. We can talk about the P.W.A. some other time, if you don't mind. Right now it's imperative that you go after those men, capture as many of them as possible. And it's even more imperative that Miss Elliot and Tim Donovan here, and I, get back to New York. So—"

"Hey!" the sergeant shouted. "You don't think I'm lettin' you people go away, do you?" He grinned. "I'm not that dumb. You may be all right, and then again you may not. You'll just have to come along with us—"

Tim Donovan started to protest. "Say! We can't—"

He stopped short as Jimmy Christopher jabbed him in the ribs.

"All right, Sergeant," Jimmy said. "Just get going."

The sergeant nodded in satisfaction. "Okay. You just trail along behind us."

HE MOTIONED to one of his troopers. "Hey, Stone, you ride in that roadster with these people, and see that they follow us. Understand? No going away to New York, or anything like that. They have to drive right behind us."

Stone saluted. "Okay, Skipper. They'll come."

He nodded to Jimmy and Diane and Tim. "You heard the skipper. I'll ride the running board—and I don't stand for any monkey-shines."

"Of course you don't," Jimmy Christopher murmured.

As he turned away to go back to the roadster, the other troopers piled back into their cars. The sergeant called after Jimmy, "Sorry, Cap, but I got to stick to regulations. If we catch any of these guys, we'll have to have you around to testify."

"Sure, sure," Jimmy said without turning, and he continued toward the roadster, with Trooper Stone walking warily alongside him.

The three State Police cars started, rolled away down the road. Tim Donovan, walking on the other side of Operator 5 from Trooper Stone, whispered to Jimmy Christopher:

"Are you really going with them, Jimmy? We're wasting valuable time. That book I gave you is in code. You should be decoding it—"

Jimmy gave the boy a jab in the ribs, and Tim quieted. Diane was walking a little in advance of them, and when she reached the car, she turned and glanced questioningly at Jimmy, who nodded to her almost imperceptibly.

She got into the car behind the wheel, then turned and flashed a smile at Trooper Stone.

"Will you sit next to me, Officer?" she asked. "I'll feel so much—safer with you beside me."

Stone expanded under her smile. "It's okay by me, Miss."

He started to climb in beside her, and Jimmy stepped up close behind him, caught both his elbows behind him with his right arm, and reached around with his left hand to yank the service revolver out of the holster hanging from the Sam Browne belt.

Before the astonished trooper realized what had happened, Jimmy gave him a little shove backward, covering him with his own revolver.

"Sorry, Stone," Jimmy Christopher said pleasantly. "We've got important business in New York. Give our apologies to the skipper, will you?"

Tim Donovan, grinning like a cat, climbed into the rumble seat, and Jimmy got in beside Diane, still covering Stone, who stood there alternately glaring at them and looking down the road after the three police cars which had already disappeared.

He exclaimed hotly, "I thought there was something phony about this whole business. If you think you're gonna get away with this, you're crazy. We'll have an alarm out for you in an hour. And boy, when you're picked up, the skipper'll give you the works!"

Jimmy smiled pleasantly. "Goodbye, Trooper Stone," he called out, "and good luck!" Tim Donovan, from the rumble seat, made a significant noise with his lips—a noise generally known as "the razzberry."

"Let 'er go, Diane!" he shouted.

Diane let the powerful motor out, and raced the car away from there.

Jimmy swung around in his seat, facing forward. His smile disappeared.

"Now, Diane," he said urgently, "drive as you never drove before!"

While the girl drove through the night toward New York, he pored over the notebook that Tim Donovan had given him....

CHAPTER 2
PLOT AND COUNTERPLOT

IN A brownstone house not far from Grand Central Terminal in New York City, a man sat at a desk in a huge, peculiarly lit room, on the top floor. The shades were all drawn on the windows. At either side of the desk were two floor lamps. They were so arranged that their light was thrown away from the desk, flooding the rest of the room, but leaving the man at the desk in deepest shadow. There were other rooms in the house....

In some of these rooms, men sat about idly, smoking foreign cigarettes and sipping Turkish coffee. In other rooms, men worked at desks; some poring over sectional maps of the United States, others at telephones and telegraph keys.

These men were of all nationalities, as their features attested. Every once in a while, one of them arose from a phone or a telegraph instrument, went upstairs and knocked respectfully at the door of the room on the top floor. He entered and delivered a message to the man who sat there alone, received terse orders in a guttural tone, and left again. Always the guttural-voiced one remained unseen behind the protection of his twin lamps, while the man who reported blinked in the glare from them.

One of these men, after knocking and being admitted, stood near the door and said, "I have just heard from the speaker on Union Square, Master. He delivered his talk, and after the meeting two converts approached him. They wish to dedicate themselves to the fight for peace. Shall he bring them here, Master?"

"No!" said the man behind the desk. "Let him bring them to sub-headquarters number five. They will remain there until they have been investigated. We must be sure they are not Intelligence agents trying to worm their way in."

The man at the door bowed. "It shall be as you say, Master." He was a thin man, with a high forehead and a fanatical gleam in his eyes. "Soon, Master," he said, "we shall not fear these agents!"

"No," repeated the Master. "You are right, Leon. Soon we shall fear no one. When our word has spread to these benighted people, they will lay away their arms forever!"

Leon backed out of the room, but returned in a few moments. "Radvik is here, Master, from sub-headquarters number two, in New Jersey. I told him that you are displeased with him. Do you wish to speak with him?"

The Master grunted. "Bring him in."

The man, Radvik, who entered, was tall, raw-boned, gaunt of face. He had a long head that sat on a scrawny neck encased in a collar several sizes too big for it. In his eyes there was the same sort of fanatical gleam that was to be observed in Leon's eyes.

Radvik took a step or two into the room, then stood still, his eyes cast toward the floor. The light from the two lamps shone into his face, showed that his mouth was twitching nervously.

"Well, Radvik," said the man behind the desk. "What have you to say for yourself?"

Radvik gulped. "Nothing, Master. Through my carelessness, the boy escaped with the book of plans."

FOR A moment there was silence, then the Master said, "Tell me everything that happened, Radvik." There was no emotion in that voice—not the slightest hint of inflection. It was as if the Master were an automaton.

Radvik hesitated, then spoke swiftly: "As you know, Master, I held a peace meeting at Columbus Circle last night. At the end of my speech I had four converts, and among them was this boy. I did not want him, for he seemed too young. But he pleaded with me, saying that he would be glad to die for the cause of peace, just as I had said I would be, in my speech. So I yielded, brought him along with the others to sub-headquarters number two, in Jersey."

He paused, glanced sideways at Leon, who stood motionless, saying nothing. Then he blinked into the glare of the two lamps, wet his lips.

The Master, virtually invisible to him behind the desk, said unemotionally, "Go on, Radvik."

Radvik spread his hands. "How was I to know, Master, that the brat was the young devil who works with that Operator 5? I took him among the other converts. As you know, Master, there were more than a hundred of them there, waiting for orders. I let him mingle with them, and I gave them a talk, explaining some of our plans. This evening the boy came into my office. Somehow he had got hold of a blackjack. And I learned later that he had sent a code message to Operator 5 over our own telegraph-sending set. He slugged me; you can still see the wound—" He indicated a white bandage on the back of his head behind the right ear. "And he went through my pockets, taking the small book of confidential plans which you gave me, Master. But he did not knock me out entirely. Just as he was escaping through the cellar, I came to, and gave chase. I brought out all the converts, and we chased him across the marshes. We would have caught him, had it not been for a car that came with a machine gun and mowed us down. The converts did not fear death. They rushed the car, but they could do nothing against the machine gun. Thirty of them died, and the car escaped with that devil of a boy. Then the State Troopers came, and we fled."

JIMMY CHRISTOPHER

He ceased talking, stood with his hands clasped before him,
as if awaiting judgment.

"So?" the man behind the desk asked softly. "Our sub-headquarters in Jersey is in the hands of the troopers?"

"Yes, Master."

"And the converts there are killed and scattered?"

"Yes, Master."

"And the book with the secret plans is in the hands of this Operator 5?"

"Y-yes, Master."

"You have failed, Radvik—failed miserably."

Radvik bowed his head. "I have failed," he repeated.

"You know the penalty of failure?"

"I—know it."

There was no sign of fear in Radvik's eyes as his hand went to his pocket, came out slowly with an automatic. Rather, there was in his face a sort of fanatical resignation.

No word was spoken in the large room. Leon made no move to stop Radvik as he raised the gun—not to point it at the man behind the desk, *but to place the muzzle against his own forehead!*

He stood that way a moment, then said, "Master, gladly do I pay the penalty—for the sake of the Cause! Master, I, who am about to die, salute you!"

And he pulled the trigger....

FOR A long time there was no sound in the room, after the echo of the revolver shot had died away. The man, Leon, shivered a bit, and glanced down at the lifeless body of Radvik, then looked up and blinked into the light.

From behind the desk came the cool, imperturbable voice of the Master: "Bring in men, Leon. Have him taken away."

Leon bowed, started for the door. And suddenly he stiffened as the sound of a weird chuckle came to him from behind the lights.

He stopped, glanced toward the desk. The Master's voice cut

like a knife through the stillness of the room. "So Operator 5 has stolen a march on me! What do you think of him, Leon?"

Leon said respectfully, "I think he is a very clever young man. And that boy who works with him is nearly as smart." He looked worried, stepped around the body of Radvik toward the door, halted with his hand on the knob. "What will you do, Master? Operator 5 will surely be able to decode the plan book. He will know what we propose—"

The Master chuckled. "What would you do in my place, Leon?"

Leon drew in his breath sibilantly. "I would try to find this Operator 5 without delay. I would seize him and take the book—"

"No, no, you fool! You see, Leon, that is why I am the Master and you are the disciple. You think only of the obvious, while I—*I* think of the devious. Don't you know, you fool, that Operator 5 will be expecting a move like that? He will have taken steps to guard himself while he decodes the book. He may even attempt to lay a trap for us."

Leon's eyes were wide. "What, then, shall we do, Master?"

"Think, Leon. This Operator is only a man like yourself. How best does one hurt a man whom one cannot reach?"

"Why—perhaps through those he loves—"

"Exactly! Now, Leon, I had you investigate this Operator 5, did I not? And though there was little to discover, you did succeed in eliciting information from that Secret Service man whom we converted, did you not?"

Leon's eyes sparkled. He forgot the bloody body almost at his feet. "That is so!"

"And what are the facts that you discovered about him?"

"He is a young man, Master, but he has seen and done much. He is old beyond his years, and a dangerous adversary. The boy, Tim Donovan, is dearly loved by him, and accompanies him almost everywhere. There is also a girl, Diane Elliot. She is a newspaper reporter, young, beautiful. It is said that Operator 5 would give his right arm for her—"

"Aha! Now you have come to it, Leon! This Diane Elliot—she goes about the city, gathering news, interviewing people. She is not protected. She can be reached. It is through her, Leon, that we shall recover our plan book—unread!"

"I see, Master," said Leon softly.

"Now go!" said the Master. "Arrange for Segurius to hold a peace meeting on Forty-second Street—tonight!"

IN THE Port Authority Building on Eighth Avenue and Thirteenth Street in the City of New York, there is a suite of offices on one of the upper floors which is very deceptive in appearance. From the name on the door, and from the ordinary activity of the few clerks in the outer offices, one would assume that this was no different from any of the numerous importing and exporting firms in New York. But once past the outer offices, a very different form of activity becomes evident.

Telautograph machines unwind strip after strip of messages from every quarter of the country. Alert, keen-eyed men arrange these messages, prepare answers, or submit them to a single man in an inner office who scans them and makes a quick decision as to what action to take in connection with them.

This man is stocky, thin-lipped, square-jawed, with flashing black eyes and black hair. Tonight he sat at his desk with a sheaf of messages in front of him, and there was weariness in every movement of him. He ruffled through the flimsies, raised haggard eyes to the portly, gray-haired man who sat opposite him.

"I tell you, sir," he exclaimed, "I can't make head or tail of this! None of my operatives has reported a single concrete fact to help me!"

The gray-haired man stirred in his seat, said urgently, "You've *got* to break this thing, and break it fast, Z-7! Do you understand what this means to the country? Our naval plans are crippled; our biggest shipyard has been wiped from the face of the earth. But that is not the worst!" He leaned forward, tapped the desk with his forefinger. "What is to prevent another rocket from being launched at another of our vulnerable spots? What"—his voice rose a bit—"is to prevent *every one* of our defenses from being demolished in like manner?"

The black-haired man shook his head, hopelessly. "I don't know, sir. We seem to be at the mercy of some unknown force, and until we discover its identity, we're up against a blank wall!"

This man, known as Z-7, was the supreme chief of the United States Secret Service—the man who had complete authority over all the Intelligence Agents in the employ of the United States. And the man he was talking to was the Secretary of the Navy, who had flown to New York from Washington for the express purpose of consulting him.

Now Z-7 fingered through the flimsies on the desk, picked one out, and studied it. Then he handed it across to the Secretary of the Navy.

"What do you think of this, sir? I received it only a few minutes before you came."

THE PORTLY man took the sheet, adjusted his glasses, and read the message. Z-7, watching him, could see the color leap to his face as its import struck him. The message was as follows:

... Z-7 ... PA-NY ... REROUTE THROUGH WDC 13 ... CAPTAIN STIKES COMMANDING SS HANSIC JUST DOCKED IN BOSTON ... REPORTS SIGHTING UNIDENTIFIED FLEET OF OCEAN LINERS FOUR HUNDRED MILES OFF COAST OF NOVA SCOTIA ... SHIPS FIRED AT HIM BUT HE ESCAPED DUE TO THICK FOG ... BELIEVES THERE WERE AT LEAST TWELVE VESSELS IN FLEET FLYING STRANGE FLAG BEARING INSIGNIA OF COILED DRAGON ... SHALL I INVESTIGATE FURTHER ... BS-1 ....

The Secretary's hand trembled as he put down the paper. "A strange fleet?" he gasped. "What can it mean? That captain must have been drunk!"

Z-7 smiled grimly. "If anybody had reported to you that Newport News was going to be wiped off the map, sir, you would have said that he was drunk, too!"

"You mean that there actually is such a fleet, approaching the United States? A fleet flying a flag with a dragon on it? Why man, there's no such flag—"

"It seems there is now, sir," Z-7 insisted. "And what's more, I'll wager you that there's another such fleet somewhere off Cuba—and it's from one of those ships that the rocket came!"

"But good God, man! That rocket deliberately veered from a westerly course to a northerly one when it reached the Florida Keys. How could that be done?"

Z-7 shrugged. "I don't know the answer to that yet, sir. I don't understand how it was able to reach Newport News unerringly—at night."

"Well—" The Secretary stopped as a knock sounded on the door. A clerk entered to announce: "Operator 5 is here, sir, with Miss Elliot and Tim Donovan."

Z-7 exclaimed eagerly, "Show him in!"

Operator 5 shook hands with Z-7 and with the Secretary of the Navy, whom he had met before. Then he introduced Diane and Tim. "We've just got here from Jersey," he explained. "Tim here, had an adventure that nearly cost him his life, but he has gotten information that gives us a definite lead to the perpetrators of the rocket atrocity at Newport News!"

The Secretary of the Navy stared at the freckle-faced Irish lad. He asked eagerly, "What sort of lead is it? God, we're at our wits' end here!"

"Tim," said Jimmy Christopher, "has obtained definite information which connects this Peace Movement that has swept the country with an undercover espionage crew. All these peace speakers mushrooming all over are nothing more than recruiters, enlisting officers for an army that is supposed to overrun the nation at the proper moment!"

"What!" exclaimed the Secretary. "All those peaceful chaps who orate against war?"

"Exactly, sir. Their business is to undermine the morale of the country, to prepare it for some sort of invasion that is corning soon. I can't quite figure what country would be the aggressor at this time, with things as they are in Europe, but I am almost positive that an invasion is being planned."

Z-7 AND the Secretary of the Navy exchanged significant glances. Z-7 handed Jimmy Christopher the flimsy containing the message from the Boston office. Jimmy read it gravely, then showed it to Diane and Tim.

"That bears me out," he said. "Whatever country owns those battleships is only awaiting the proper time to strike. In the meantime, they are breaking down our national defenses so that we will be unable to offer any effectual resistance when they land."

"But," blurted the Secretary of the Navy, "this is unthinkable! To be attacked by an unknown power—"

"The tragedy at Newport News, sir," Jimmy told him, "will not be the last. There'll be one after the other, now—"

"But what can we do to stop it?"

Jimmy shrugged. He produced the little red notebook which

30

Tim had given him. "This may contain the war plans of the attackers. When I decode it, I'll probably have information about who they are as well as what they intend to do. But it'll take me hours to find the key. I'm going to work on it right now."

"And what'll we do in the meantime?" the Secretary groaned. "Those battleships may swoop down on our coast at any moment. If they control any more rockets like the one that struck Newport News, they'll be able to wipe out our fleet—"

"I suggest," said Jimmy quietly, "that you make use of the new electrical depth-mines which you were preparing for the defense of the Panamá Canal. Have them placed at a distance from our coastline, in a position to protect our larger harbors. If that mysterious fleet should attempt to land, they would naturally choose a large harbor—"

"How," the secretary asked in a queer tone, "did you know about those new depth-mines? They were a navy secret!"

Jimmy Christopher exchanged a glance with Z-7 and smiled. "There are a lot of things, sir, that Intelligence knows, which are supposed to be secrets. I know that you've ordered five hundred of them, and that they're ready for delivery now. You couldn't put them to better use than to protect our coastline."

"I'll attend to it at once!" the Secretary said. "I'll have every factory that's making them ship them out at once—without delay. Now, about these peace speakers. You, Z-7, should round up every mother's son of them up. Put them behind bars—"

"No, no!" Jimmy broke in. "That would be fatal!" He lowered his voice. "You see, sir, these speakers are nothing but cat's-paws. They're fanatics who've been converted to the cause of peace by some sinister mastermind who is using them for his own purposes. To arrest them would profit us nothing. We must let them carry on their meetings, and we must keep a close watch on them. Eventually, they will lead us to this master of theirs. He is the one we want—not these duped fanatics."

"But I don't understand," said the Secretary of the Navy. "What do these men hope to gain for peace by opening this country to foreign invasion?"

JIMMY SMILED enigmatically. "They have nothing to gain. But they have listened to a magnetic orator. Their master must have an overpowering personality. He has sold them on the theory that it is better to die than to plunge humanity into another war."

"Bosh! You can sell a man a lot of ideas, but you can't sell him on dying!"

"I can show you where you are mistaken, sir," Jimmy said quietly. "Take the rocket that struck Newport News, for instance. Have you been able to figure out how it was that it veered in its course over the Florida Keys, and turned northward?"

"No, I haven't. But what has that to do—?"

"I'll tell you, sir. That rocket found its mark so unerringly, *because there was a living man inside to guide it!*"

The black eyes of Z-7 suddenly flashed with understanding. "God!" he exclaimed. "I never thought of that!"

"You see," Jimmy went on, "the man who guided that torpedo through the air gave his life to destroy our shipyards. The diabolical master of this campaign has filled these converts of his with such enthusiasm that they deem their lives worth nothing compared with the success of the great cause of Peace for which they believe they are fighting. You should have seen those men on the Jersey marshes rush against our machine gun. They knew they would be mowed down, yet they came on. If we hadn't driven away in the car, they would have gotten to us. Dozens of them died—willingly."

The Secretary of the Navy looked at Jimmy Christopher somberly. "If what you say is true, Operator 5, we are fighting against almost hopeless odds—"

"Not," Jimmy Christopher corrected him, "entirely hopeless. I hope that we'll find a way to beat this master of theirs yet. This book should yield some vital information. We should be able to get at their other headquarters by shadowing their speakers—"

Diane stepped forward, her eyes shining eagerly. "I have an idea, Jimmy! There's going to be one of those peace meetings on Forty-second Street tonight. I'll go there and interview the speaker. I've already been given that assignment to cover for the Amalgamated Press, so it'll look entirely natural—"

Jimmy Christopher frowned. "I'd rather you didn't, Diane. It's dangerous—"

Diane's eyes snapped. "You let Tim risk his life, didn't you? You risk your own every day. If you don't think I'm as capable as Tim—"

"It's not that, Diane," Jimmy replied, and she flushed at the warmth that shone in his eyes. "It's not that, and you know it. If anything happened to you—"

"I'd feel as bad if anything happened to you. Yet I don't urge you to stay away from danger when you have to go!"

Reluctantly, Jimmy nodded. "All right, Diane, you win. But be careful. Z-7, will you send a couple of men after her, in case she gets in trouble?"

"Gladly!" said Z-7.

"What about me?" Tim Donovan asked. "Suppose I—?"

"You, Tim," said Jimmy firmly, "are coming home with me and get some sleep while I decode this book. And no arguments!"

CHAPTER 3
HOSTAGE TO DOOM

"**A**ND I say to you that the Master's words are a living fire that shall drench this land in a bath of blood! Your cities shall be toppled over as were Sodom and Gomorrah! Your arsenals and your forts and your navies shall feel upon them the pallid breath of destruction, and they shall wither away before the death-blasts of the Master!"

The words, spoken oratorically, with fire and with energy, rang loud above the rumble of the Saturday night traffic of New York City on Forty-second Street.

The speaker stood upon a platform under the elevated viaduct that carried automobile traffic from Fourth Avenue up around the Grand Central Terminal and into Park Avenue, two blocks north.

The trolley car tracks which had formerly run under the

viaduct here had recently been removed; the trolley line had been replaced by a bus system. And the space under the viaduct, right at the corner of Forty-second Street and directly opposite Grand Central Terminal, was now given over to outdoor speakers for queer causes. Here, at different times of the day for which their permits were granted, could be heard Communist orators, Seventh-Day Adventists, Atheists, Share-the-Wealth pleaders, and a various assortment of exponents of odd *"isms"* and *"ologies."*

Tonight's speaker was a tall, gaunt man with a dark face and broad features that were almost Negroid. His eyes were deep-set under thick, shaggy brows. He was dressed in a manner to attract attention even in blasé New York.

He wore a pair of khaki breeches, tied at the waist with a rope. He was barefooted, and his only other articles of clothing were a gray vest, open in front, and a soiled white turban wound about his head. The vest left his chest and arms bare. The skin of his torso was dark, like his face, and there was no hair on his chest. His lips, unlike the rest of his features, were thin, constantly turned down at the corners.

As he spoke, in a powerful voice that carried almost across the wide street in spite of the traffic noises, white teeth flashed behind those lips. His arms and chest rippled with corded muscles. He might have been an Ethiopian warrior or a Hindu fanatic. The hundred or two people who crowded around him, listening, didn't know exactly what he was preaching. But a New York crowd is always willing to give ear to something new, and this was new.

The speaker raised his arm, with a finger pointing upward to heaven, and roared at the crowd: "Destruction and death shall come unto you who use the weapons of war! Throw away your guns and your bombs and your flying machines and your ships of war before it is too late. For as surely as you live by steel, so shall you all perish by steel! My master has said it, and he has sent me forth to tell you. Your weapons shall be as naught, when the Doom comes upon you!"

He continued, and his voice rose in a fanatical scream. His deep eyes blazed, and his fists clenched in the air as if he were hurling curses at the throng.

"Already your proud ships of war have been struck by the lightning wrath of the heavens. You are a misguided, wicked people, and you have been building a Tower of Babel to the God of War. But the God of Peace has looked down upon you, and has blasted your infamous tower with a single breath. Beware! Anger him not further!"

AS THE speaker continued, a taxicab drew up at the corner, and Diane Elliot descended from it. Her lively blue eyes scanned the crowd, studied the speaker. She glanced behind her, saw that another taxicab had stopped a little way back, and that the two Intelligence agents whom Z-7 had assigned to her were getting out of it. She gave them no sign of recognition, but moved into the crowd around the fanatical speaker.

By this time, the crowd which had come to jeer was staying to listen in all seriousness. For there is nothing that impresses the average New Yorker so much as evident sincerity. He meets it so seldom in his daily life that it strikes him between the eyes when he does encounter it.

And this gaunt, raw-boned speaker was quite evidently sincere. He believed every word that he spoke; he believed that the destruction which he threatened would surely overtake his listeners. His powerful voice hammered home to them each direful prophecy.

Diane edged forward into the center of the crowd, gazing up at the speaker as she did so. She found it hard to believe that this man who looked like an ascetic was in reality the agent of some foreign power planning destruction and death for the country.

Behind her, the two Intelligence agents pushed through the crowd, separating and trying to appear as inconspicuous as possible. They did not know that their every move was being observed; that dark, baleful eyes were fixed continuously upon their backs.

From the fringes of the crowd, half a dozen men moved in after the agents. These men were small, wiry, and their eyes burned with hatred.

The meeting lasted for perhaps fifteen minutes longer, and then the speaker suddenly raised his hands high above him, as if flinging a benediction or a curse at the crowd. He shouted, "I have talked enough. I will not say more unto you. I have spoken the Master's word, and you that heed not shall perish! But you others who wish for peace as I do, come forward to me. Let me look into your eyes, and hold your hand, and call you brother. And like brothers let us *fight* for *peace!*"

He stepped down from the rostrum, and men crowded around him, carried away by the power of his oratory. He stood there, tall and gaunt, towering over the others, not feeling the biting cold, though he wore scant clothing.

Diane pushed through those about him, touched his shoulder. He turned, stared at her for a moment, inquiringly. "I am from the Amalgamated Press," she told him. "I've been sent here to get an interview with you. I wonder if you could spare me a few minutes?"

He frowned, appeared to be about to refuse, then suddenly nodded. "Come," he said. "I will give you an interview."

He took her arm, and Diane winced at the strength of him. He led her out of the small crowd about him, saying impatiently to them, "You who wish to hear more, come back tomorrow night. Tomorrow I will tell you what you must do to avoid doom!"

He cleared a way for Diane and himself roughly, led her to the car parked just behind the box upon which he had been speaking. A dark man sat at the wheel of this car, and he handed Diane into it, got in beside her.

Now that he was so close to her, she felt rather repelled by him. There was a strange, mad light in his eyes, and she saw that his lips curled cruelly. In the close interior of the car she got the unwashed odor of his body, and it almost nauseated her. But she managed to smile and said, "First of all, of course, I suppose I should ask your name."

He nodded, without smiling. "I am Segurius."

"I am Diane Elliot," she answered. "Can you tell me how you became interested in this peace movement?"

"Easily. I listened to the words of the Master, and I saw

what there was to be done. None who listen to the Master can fail to believe!"

"Who is this master of yours, Segurius?" she asked innocently.

HIS LIPS twitched, and he leaned closer to her, so that the smell of him became even stronger. His voice sounded sonorous, reverent. "He is the one who shall bring true peace to the world! By fire and the sword he will bring peace to the world! God has given him the power to destroy the pillars of war, and he will destroy them. Would you like to listen to the Master yourself?"

Diane felt her blood race. "I'd love to!" she said.

For a long moment he looked at her, as if measuring her, appraising her. "I warn you," he spoke slowly, "that when you have listened, you will change. You will be your own mistress no longer. You will have the urge to fight for this cause, and nothing that you may do will free you. Whoever hears the Master's voice is forever bound by it!"

He saw the hint of doubt in her eyes, and he laughed shortly. "You doubt? You think that you can resist the message of the Master! Then you are a fool! Many have doubted. But all have been converted. I tell you that when you have heard the Master, you will believe."

Diane stole a glance out of the rear window of the car, saw

that the two Intelligence agents were standing close by. They had hailed a taxicab, which was now pulled up a little way from Segurius' car, ready to start as soon as he did.

Diane swung her eyes back to Segurius, met his gaze squarely. "I still want to meet your Master," she said firmly.

Segurius' lips clamped tightly. There was a fierce look of triumph in them. "So be it!" he said.

As if his words had been a signal, the chauffeur threw the car into gear, started it off, heading south.

Behind them, the two Intelligence agents started to get into their cab. One of them said to the driver, "Follow that sedan. Keep a little behind it, but don't lose it!" He flashed a government badge as he spoke, and the cabby nodded, reached around to close the door.

And just then, a half-dozen wiry shapes swarmed about the cab, darted inside, leaped upon the two agents. The Intelligence men, taken by surprise, went for their guns. But they didn't have a chance. Steel flashed in the air, descended swiftly, viciously. Blood spurted from a dozen wounds as the two agents slumped on the upholstery, dead.

The driver, ashen of face, opened his mouth to shout, but a blade sliced through the air, slashed across his throat. A passerby saw it, and shouted, "Police!"

Men and women turned, stared, shocked, while the wiry shapes darted away across the street into the subway entrance, to disappear.

The uniformed policeman came running from the corner. A

crowd assembled. But the agents were dead, and their assailants were gone.

And the car with Diane and Segurius swung east at Fortieth Street, then north again at Third Avenue, then east once more on Forty-second. At First Avenue, it turned south once more, sped past several corners, turned into a side street, and pulled up before a brownstone house.

Segurius smiled at Diane for the first time, showing two rows of broken, discolored teeth. "Come," he said. "You shall see the Master!"

Diane descended from the car, glanced backward to see if the agents had followed them. She saw several taxicabs, but could not be sure which one was theirs. She felt a momentary twinge of doubt at the thought that perhaps they had lost her, but she shrugged it off. Those two agents were among the most experienced in the Service. They were no doubt in one of the passing cars and would have this house spotted....

SHE WENT with Segurius to the street-level door of the brownstone, waited while he rang the bell. A head appeared for a moment at an upper window, peering down. Then the door was opened, and they passed inside.

The man who admitted them was thin, with a high forehead. He looked at Diane curiously, but indicated no surprise at seeing her there. Segurius spoke no word to this man, yet he turned and led them up two flights of stairs, as if he knew just what was wanted of him.

Diane glanced about her at the closed doors that they passed. She could hear sounds of activity from behind those doors; she knew that there were many people in this house. Yet suddenly, inexplicably, she felt herself shivering.

She looked up at Segurius, who was walking beside her, behind the man who had admitted them, and she saw that Segurius was watching her, smiling in a queer sort of way. She clamped her jaws firmly, walked on until they reached the door of a room on the top floor.

Their guide knocked respectfully on this door, and a guttural voice from within said, "Yes?"

"It is she whom you expect, Master."

"Let her come in, Leon—alone!"

The guide bowed to her, placed his hand on the knob of the door.

"The Master," he said to her, "will talk to you. He has instructed me to tell you in advance that he has decided to show himself to you—a thing which he rarely does. But he has decided to do so now, so that when you write about him, you may tell your readers who and what he really is."

TIM DONOVAN

There was a sardonic gleam in the man's eyes as he pushed open the door and stood aside for Diane to enter. She glanced back at Segurius, saw that he, too, was smiling queerly, twistedly.

She felt an irresistible impulse to turn back, to flee from this house. But she mastered it, turning to face the room....

Through the open doorway she saw the desk at the far end, saw the shape of the man behind the desk. But she could distinguish nothing more, for the two powerful lights shining on either side of the desk practically blinded her, made it impossible to distinguish more than the vague outline of the man.

Steeling herself, she stepped into the room, and the door closed behind her. The guttural voice from behind the desk asked, "You are Diane Elliot?"

She nodded, blinking into the light, her pupils contracting.

"You have come to see the Master?"

Once more she nodded. She gulped. That voice was so ominous, so sinister. If she had wanted to talk at the moment, she felt that she would not have been able to.

"Good!" said the voice behind the desk. "You shall see the Master. Look!"

The two powerful lights were extinguished. The room was cast into total darkness. Diane felt a cold sensation along her spine, as she stood there, seeing nothing.

Then, a small night light sprang into life on the desk. Its glow was dull, but it illumined the features of the man behind the desk.

Diane looked. Her eyes dilated with terror and dread. Her body shivered. And she screamed. She screamed again and again, her voice rising to an unbearable pitch of hysteria, until her vocal cords could no longer stand the strain. Then her body buckled, and she slumped to the floor in a dead faint.

Almost at once, the night light was switched out, and the two powerful floor lamps burst into brilliant light. From behind the desk there came a fiendish chuckle....

CHAPTER 4
TIM'S TREASON

IN THE Port Authority Building, Jimmy Christopher sat at a desk in a secluded room of the Intelligence Offices, poring over the little red notebook which Tim had given him.

He was applying to the code all the tests with which he was familiar, in an effort to break it down. His knowledge of code work was wide. He had done some notable work in the Black Chamber; it had become a watchword that there was no code in existence that Operator 5 could not break down. This one was not too difficult, but it was a very unwieldy one, and Jimmy could see that it would take five or six hours more to work out the proper formula.

Behind him, on a couch, Tim Donovan slept the sleep of exhaustion. His experience on the Jersey marshes had left him weak and tired.

A rap sounded on the door, and Z-7 entered. Jimmy looked up, smiled. "It's only a matter of time, Chief. This book should give us the lowdown on the power behind this whole business."

Z-7 nodded. "Keep at it, Jimmy. In the meantime, the Secretary of the Navy has followed all of your suggestions. He has ordered Admiral Ernst of the Atlantic Fleet to investigate those ships that were sighted by the captain of the *Hansic*. The depth mines are being loaded into army trucks and rushed to the Brooklyn Navy Yard to be transferred to three mine-layers. By tomorrow night, the coastline will be protected at every important harbor—"

He stopped as voices sounded from the outer office and turned as a clerk entered. The clerk said to Z-7, "We've just had word from police headquarters, sir. L-9 and P-18 were stabbed to death twenty minutes ago, on Forty-second Street!"

Z-7 went white at the news. He waved the clerk out of the room, then turned to look, haggard-eyed, at Jimmy. Operator 5 arose with quick sympathy, placing a hand on Z-7's shoulder.

"Stabbed!" he muttered. "I knew both those boys. Why—?"

Suddenly he stopped, as a terrible thought struck him. "Chief!" he exclaimed. "L-9 and P-18—were they the men you assigned—?"

He saw the truth in Z-7's eyes as his chief nodded bitterly. "Yes, Jimmy. They were assigned to protect Diane. I'm afraid—"

Jimmy Christopher's fists clenched at his sides. He turned to find Tim, fully awake now, sitting up on the couch and staring at him with wide eyes. "Jimmy!" Tim said very low. "They've—got Diane?"

Operator 5 nodded, said huskily, "I'm going out and find her!" He pushed blindly past Z-7, who made no effort to stop him.

Z-7 glanced at the notebook lying on the desk, but said nothing. Tim got up to follow him. "I'm going with you, Jimmy!"

But at the doorway, Operator 5 stopped. A clerk from the telegraph room was hurrying down the hall, white-faced, with a sheaf of yellow flimsies. The clerk's hand shook as he extended them to Z-7, saying, "These came in so fast, sir, I took them all down before bringing them. It's—awful, sir!"

Z-7 said to Operator 5, "Wait, Jimmy. Perhaps—"

He read the first one, said under his breath: "Good God!

46

They're striking again!" He passed the first one to Jimmy, read the next and the next, handing them over as he read them.

The first one was from the Portsmouth office. It read as follows:

> ... PA-NY... FORTS FOSTER LEVETT AND LYON DESTROYED BY ROCKETS SIMULTANEOUSLY AT TEN-FIVE P.M. EASTERN STANDARD TIME... FIRE SPREADING... NINE THOUSAND MEN KILLED... ROCKETS APPEARED FROM DIRECTION OF ATLANTIC OCEAN... PS-1....

The next, also from Portsmouth:

> ... FORT MCKINLEY AND FORT PREBLE DESTROYED BY ROCKETS AT TEN-TEN P.M. EASTERN STANDARD TIME... SIX THOUSAND LIVES LOST... HOW CAN WE PROTECT NAVAL STATION HERE... PS-1....

JIMMY CHRISTOPHER raised his eyes to Z-7. "They're destroying our coast defenses, Chief! You know what this means—we won't have a gun or a man left on the coast when they land. And we don't even know who they are!"

"Here," said Z-7 tightly. "Read this one."

It was an unfinished message from Portsmouth:

> ... ROCKET STRUCK NAVAL STATION HERE IN PORTSMOUTH AT TEN-FOURTEEN... U.S.S. TRIPOLI AND U.S.S. BANGOR ALSO DESTROYED

IN EXPLOSION… BUILDINGS HERE IN PORTS-
MOUTH CRUMBLING FROM SHOCK… AFRAID
CITY GOING… S.O.…

"My God!" said Z-7, thumbing through the other flimsies.
"Every one of our forts and naval stations is going. We'll be absolutely defenseless. Here, look at these others—Fort Andrews,
Fort Banks, Fort Constitution, Fort Greble—" He stopped,
pallid-faced. "Jimmy! They're crippling New England!"

Jimmy nodded tightly. "It means that the invasion will come
through there. Those ships that were sighted along Nova Scotia
must be full of men, ready to land—"

Another clerk hurried in with a message which he handed to
Z-7. It was from Bangor, Maine. Jimmy read it over his chief's
shoulder, with Tim Donovan crowding beside him:

… PA-NY… STRANGE SHIPS SIGHTED OFF
PENOBSCOT BAY… PUTTING OFF ARMED MEN IN
BOATS… WE HAVE NO FACILITIES FOR DEFENSE
LEFT… FOR GOD'S SAKE SEND PLANES… SHIPS
ARE FLYING QUEER FLAG WITH A COILED
DRAGON… WE DON'T KNOW WHAT COUNTRY
THEY ARE… BR-1.…

Z-7 exclaimed: "It's come! We're being invaded, and Intelligence is caught flat-footed. We don't even know our enemy!"
He turned to one of the clerks. "Wilkins! Phone the Secretary
of War! Have him order every available plane to the coast of
Maine! We've—"

Jimmy put a hand on Z-7's sleeve. "That won't help, Chief. I can tell you what their next step is going to be. They'll threaten to destroy Bangor and the other big cities in New England if we offer resistance. We can't have that happen. We've got to let them advance for the time being!"

Z-7 stared at Jimmy. "Let them advance! Man, you're crazy! We've got to fight We—!"

Another clerk hurried down the hall toward them, announced: "Washington on the phone, sir. Will you take it in here?"

Z-7 nodded, picked up the extension phone in the room, talked into it.

Jimmy Christopher and Tim Donovan were left staring at each other. In the minds of both were the same thoughts: *What of Diane, in the hands of the unknown enemy?*

In a moment, Z-7 turned from the phone, still keeping the line open. He covered the mouthpiece with his hand. "It's the Secretary of State," he said. "A message has just been received. It was mailed by special delivery this afternoon—*before* the coast bombardment began. It states that all troops must be withdrawn from the states of Maine, New Hampshire, Massachusetts, Connecticut and Rhode Island at once. If the evacuation is not begun immediately, Bangor, Concord, Boston and Providence will be destroyed by rockets before midnight! You were right about their strategy, Jimmy. What are we to do?"

Jimmy Christopher nodded grimly, strode across the room to Z-7. "We must evacuate, Chief! There's no alternative. Until we discover how to combat these rockets, we've got to fall back— use the same defense that the primitive Ethiopians used against the modern weapons of Italy!"

"But—" stammered Z-7 "—what about our planes, our big guns? We could blast those ships out of the ocean—"

Jimmy smiled tightly. "Our planes, Chief, and our big guns are just as primitive now against those rockets as the antiquated rifles of the Ethiopians against the modern equipment of the Italian army!" He shook his head. "No. You must insist that Washington order immediate evacuation!"

Z-7 STARED at Jimmy for a long moment, still holding his hand over the receiver. Then he exclaimed under his breath, "I'm afraid you're right again, Jimmy—damn right!" And he turned, to speak meaningfully into the instrument.

Tim Donovan had been gazing at Operator 5, twisting his hands in anxiety. Now he plucked his sleeve, asking, "Jimmy! What about Diane? What are you going to do about finding her?"

The muscles of Jimmy Christopher's jaw bulged as he clamped his teeth hard. "We've—got to—forget about her, kid, for the time being. With these rockets pouring destruction down over the country, I've got to get to work on that notebook—find out what all their plans are, figure out a way to counteract them." His eyes met the boy's. "You understand, Tim?" he said hoarsely, bitterly. "It's part of being in the Service!"

Tim lowered his eyes before those of Jimmy Christopher. "You're—you're leaving Diane to her fate? You don't care—?"

"Damn!" The word exploded from Operator 5's lips as he swung away from Tim. He turned to face the wall, while Z-7 still talked into the phone.

"God, Tim! How can you say anything like that? You know how I—"

The boy's freckled face expressed sudden contrition. He stepped forward impulsively, put a hand on Operator 5's shoulder. "I'm sorry, Jimmy. I didn't mean that. I—know how you feel about Diane, and I just couldn't believe that you'd leave her—"

Z-7 hung up the phone, turned a perspired face to them. "I've convinced Washington, Jimmy," he said, "that your suggestion is the only one to follow. They're issuing orders for complete evacuation of New England. I told the Secretary of State that you're at work decoding that plan book, and that once you've got the code broken down, we may learn something about the nature of the rockets. He gave me twelve hours. At the end of twelve hours, the President is going to order all the forces of the United States against the invaders regardless of what happens to the cities threatened."

He put a hand on Jimmy's shoulder. "It's up to you, my boy, to break down that code. Get to work." He hesitated, then added falteringly, "About Diane, Jimmy. I'm going to put a dozen of our best men on the trail. They'll surely be able to accomplish as much as you could."

Jimmy Christopher gulped, then turned toward the desk and the notebook. He said nothing.

Z-7 motioned to Tim Donovan to come out of the room with him, and Tim cast a last look back at Jimmy before starting out. But at the doorway they halted. A clerk was approaching, conducting a uniformed patrolman to the room. The patrolman saluted, took an envelope from his pocket, and said, "This letter was left at headquarters by a blind beggar, sir. He was told to deliver it to us."

Z-7 looked puzzled as he took the envelope. "Why bring it here—?"

He frowned as he read the superscription on the envelope:

> Police Department:
> Please deliver this letter at once to the headquarters of the United States Intelligence Service. It is to be opened only by Operator 5!

Z-7 thanked the officer, turned and said, "Here, Jimmy. It's for you."

Jimmy Christopher got up wearily, took the envelope. "I think I've got the key to that code, Chief," he said. "It's a simple—"

He had slitted the envelope, holding it far away from him by instinct, in case it contained a form of poisonous gas or powder, and he was now reading the note enclosed. He stopped in mid-sentence, his eyes blazing as they scanned the few lines of writing.

Tim Donovan asked, "What is it, Jimmy?"

OPERATOR 5 said nothing as he silently extended the

note to Z-7, who took it and held it so that Tim could read it with him:

Operator 5:

You have a certain small notebook belonging to me. I have a certain young lady in whom you are interested. The notebook is inanimate; it has no fingernails that can be torn from its fingers, no soft flesh to be burned with hot needles, no pretty eyes to be gouged out. You are clever, Operator 5, so you gather my meaning. I want the notebook. I suggest a fair exchange. DELIVER THE BOOK TO ME AT ONCE, and the girl will be released unharmed. Send that boy of yours with the book to the corner of Fourteenth Street and Seventh Avenue. My men will know him. Act quickly. Your time is short.

—The Master of the Dragon.

Z-7 finished reading that amazing letter and emitted a deep sigh. The police officer and the clerk had left, and Z-7 fidgeted, trying to avoid looking at Jimmy Christopher. Finally he said, still not looking at Operator 5, "We've got to keep that book, Jimmy—no matter what it costs."

He had to raise his eyes then, and he shuddered at the sight of the torture in Jimmy Christopher's suddenly dull stare.

"Yes," Jimmy repeated almost mechanically. "We've—got to—keep that book." His voice almost broke on the last word, and he closed his eyes hard.

Z-7 stepped close to him, saying softly: "Nothing I can say will do any good, Jimmy boy. Except this—I'm sure Diane would want you to—carry on."

"Yes!" Jimmy exclaimed bitterly. "Carry on! That's the word! With that damnable fiend hinting at what he'll do to her!"

"I know how you feel, Jimmy," Z-7 said, very low. "You have often placed yourself in danger of death—and worse—in the service of your country. So have I. On occasion we have not hesitated to sacrifice the lives of men and even women, where the preservation of the country demanded it. I have told you often—"

"Yes, yes!" Jimmy interrupted hotly. "You've told me often that we are only numbers in the Service; that we must have no feeling, no emotion. That we must be cold automatons. But good God"—he clenched his hands hard—"we're men, Chief! Men of flesh and blood. And it's Diane—Diane that's going to be tortured, killed—!"

Suddenly he stopped, as he saw the compassionate look in Z-7's eyes. He swallowed hard, lowered his eyes. "I'm sorry, Chief. You're right. I—I'll get back—to work!"

He turned with heavy feet toward the desk, then pulled up short, his eyes widening in amazement.

"The notebook!" he said hoarsely. "It's gone!"

Z-7 stepped to his side. "I saw it there, only a few—!"

"Tim!" Jimmy Christopher interrupted him, whirling. "Tim! Where are you?"

Tim Donovan was gone. So was the notebook. The two men's eyes met in a long gaze of understanding. Z-7 said:

"Damn that boy! He's gone to deliver the book!" But there was no vindictiveness in his tone....

A KNOCK sounded on the door, and it opened at once. The

54

Secretary of the Navy, who had taken up temporary headquarters in this suite, stood on the threshold.

He glanced at the two men, standing there so tensely, and asked, "What's the matter? Have you got that book decoded yet? Better work quick. I've been on the wire to Washington, and the Secretary of State tells me he gave you twelve hours to get action."

The Secretary stopped, glancing warily from one to the other. "What's the matter with you two? You look pale as death, Z-7!"

Z-7 gulped and said, "Mr. Secretary, we haven't got that book anymore!"

"What?"

Z-7 showed him the letter from the one who signed himself the Master of the Dragon, then rapidly told him what had happened.

"It's treason!" the Secretary thundered. "Treason, I tell you! That boy should never have been permitted to assist you, Operator 5!"

"May I remind you, sir," Jimmy countered dryly, "that it was Tim Donovan who got that book in the first place. Had it not been for him—"

"That makes no difference at all, Operator 5, and you know it. Even though the boy secured the book in the first place, that does not make it his personal property. It is the property of the United States of America! What have you done to stop him?"

"Nothing yet—"

"Nothing?" the Secretary exploded. " 'Nothing!' he says! Get out of my way!" He pushed Z-7 unceremoniously aside and

The machine gun burst into life,

felling the policemen!

made for the phone. "I'll handle this myself!" He snatched up the instrument, asked for police headquarters.

He identified himself, issued terse instructions. "Radio cars to Fourteenth Street and Seventh Avenue—a freckle-faced boy—trying to deliver a notebook—must be stopped at all costs—even if you have to shoot him—work quick—only minutes to spare!"

While the Secretary was barking his orders into the phone, Jimmy whispered to Z-7: "I'm going, Chief. Maybe I can catch up to Tim." He pressed his chief's hand and then slipped from the room.

"Good luck to you, Jimmy!" Z-7 breathed after him.

CHAPTER 5
THE MASTER'S FACE

NEW YORK, at ten thirty-five p.m., was no longer a city of rushing men and women hurrying in search of evening relaxation. Army trucks rumbled through the streets—trucks with tarpaulins spread over the tops, effectively concealing their contents—trucks with a military guard, with machine guns mounted on tripods on the roofs of the cabs, each with two privates crouched and ready to let loose at the first hint of interference.

These trucks contained the newly finished depth-mines which had been destined for the Panamá Canal, but were now being expressed to the Brooklyn Navy Yard to be loaded onto mine-layers.

Such few people as were still in the streets stopped to stare at the trucks, speculating on their contents. Moodily, morosely, New Yorkers went about their business; and that business had to be mighty important to bring them out. For radios in millions of homes throughout the country had already apprised the public of the dreadful catastrophe that had struck the nation's defenses; had already announced the presence of the strange fleet of ships off the coast of Maine, and of the landing parties coming ashore unopposed.

At Fourteenth Street and Seventh Avenue, one of the army trucks was stalled at the northwest corner. The driver and the sergeant in charge of the detail were looking under the hood, while the other two privates remained up above, hunched over their machine gun.

At the southeast corner, a sedan was parked. The figures of several dark, wiry men could be distinguished within.

A police radio car raced west across Fourteenth Street, pulling up at the corner with squealing brakes. The two uniformed policemen got out of the car, their service revolvers in their hands. They stood, tense, their eyes studying everything on the corner. Another radio car roared down Seventh Avenue, made a complete turn at the corner, and pulled up alongside the first one. Its occupants also got out, revolvers in hand, to join the others.

The radios in both cars were still going. The voice of the announcer at headquarters carried to the four officers while they stood beside the coupés:

"Special call! Cars eighteen, fifteen, thirteen, twelve—go to Fourteenth Street and Seventh Avenue. Prevent a boy from delivering a book to anyone at that corner. This is government business. The boy must be stopped at all costs. Shoot, if necessary. You are dealing with dangerous foreign spies. Take no chances. I will repeat. Special—"

The officers exchanged glances. "We're first on the scene," one of them said. "What about that sedan parked across the street?"

"I'm going over and see who they are," another said. "Cover me, boys."

He started across, and just then Tim Donovan came out of the subway station on the southeast corner....

THE BOY saw the policemen and stood there at the head of the stairs, uncertainly. The door of the sedan at the curb opened and a small, dark man stepped out, heading for Tim. The police officer, halfway across the street, shouted: "Hey, you!" and raised his revolver. His three companions also started across at a run.

The dark man paid them no attention at all, acting as if they did not exist. His eyes burned into Tim's as he asked, "You are the boy with the book—no?"

Tim nodded, breathlessly, and putting his hand into his pocket, he drew out the little red notebook. The uniformed officer was drawing a bead on the wiry man, while the others, behind him, were fanning out toward the sedan. Suddenly, from behind them, came a dreadful chattering....

The machine gun on the cab of the army truck had burst into life. Slugs ricocheted on the pavement all about the policemen. The foremost one, who had been about to shoot the wiry man, fell, his body riddled with lead, his revolver unfired. The other three policemen retreated in panic, but the two pseudo-privates at the machine gun swung its wicked snout in an arc, mowing them down before they had taken a half-dozen steps backward.

A small crowd of civilians who had gathered at the unusual scene fled in panic, and the street was left deserted.

The dark, wiry man stretched out a hand, seized the notebook from Tim, and sprang back into the sedan. Tim shouted:

"Say! Where's Diane?" His youthful face twisting in anxiety, he leaped after the sedan, which roared away from the curb after the army truck, which had already started to roll.

The shade of the rear window of the sedan was down, and Tim sprang, unobserved, to the spare tire on the rear, clinging to it as the car gained speed.

The army truck raced up Seventh Avenue, turned east at Fifteenth Street against the traffic arrow. The sedan turned west, disappeared with Tim clinging to it.

And it was at that precise moment that Jimmy Christopher emerged from the subway station. He had been only one train behind Tim, but he was too late. He stared at the bodies of the dead policemen, searched in vain for Tim. His eyes clouded. This would be the end for the rash boy. No power on earth could save him from punishment now, after having virtually caused the deaths of four policemen. Perhaps, thought Jimmy bitterly, it wouldn't matter. If Tim was not here now, it could mean only that he had been carried off by the men to whom he had delivered the book—with what intentions, he could not tell.

Another radio car sped into Seventh Avenue, screeched to a stop at the curb. With heavy feet Jimmy Christopher approached it. It was his duty now to send out an alarm for Tim. If he didn't do it, it would be done by Z-7 or the enraged Secretary of the Navy. On the face of things, Tim had committed an unpardonable act of treason—punishable by a firing squad. But Jimmy Christopher could not find it in his heart to condemn the boy entirely....

IN THE brownstone house in the forties, the two lights still burned on either side of the desk behind which sat the Master. The room on the top floor was quiet, except for a slight scraping sound coming from the direction of the desk, behind those two glaring lights.

A knock sounded at the door. It opened without a word being spoken, and a woman entered.

She was perhaps five-feet, six-inches in height; her body was lithe, and she moved with a sinuous grace which was accentuated by her tight-fitting, deep-red gown that trailed the floor. The dress was cut very low, revealing the gleaming white skin of her throat and bosom. A string of pearls encircled that throat—a string that scintillated in the glare of the two lamps. Long earrings hung almost to her white shoulders, and a diamond pin glinted in the thick, black hair which was coiled high on her head.

Black, flashing eyes stared unblinking into the luminance of the lamps, and she seemed to shudder almost imperceptibly as she approached the desk. Her lips—full, red and seductive—moved as she spoke:

"The girl is awake now," she said in English, with no trace of accent. "But the shock of seeing you seems to have been too much for her. She is babbling, delirious."

The familiar, low chuckle sounded from behind the desk. "That is not surprising, my dear Zara. I—er—flatter myself that few people can stand the shock of first seeing me. Even you, dearest Zara—"

Zara closed her eyes, shuddered. But she stood straight, facing the desk. "What do you intend to do with the girl?" she asked.

The man behind the desk laughed—unpleasantly.

"You are curious, Zara? Perhaps—jealous?"

"Jealous!" Zara's eyes seemed to reflect some live dread. "I—!"

"There-there, Zara, dear. Never mind. I'll tell you what I intend. Tonight we leave for New England. The forces of the dragon are occupying the whole fertile territory of the Northeast, unopposed. There we shall set up our empire. And from there we shall conquer the world, my dear Zara—you and I!"

"And the girl?" Zara persisted.

"The girl! Ah, yes, the girl!" The voice of the unseen man took on a low edge of cunning. "I shall have another little talk with her, and then I shall send her back to Operator 5. The Master always keeps his word, Zara. If the book is delivered according to my instructions, he shall have her back. Otherwise—" the low chuckle came again "—otherwise—well, we shall see!"

Zara continued to stare into the blinding brilliance of the lights. In her eyes there was a queer look of revulsion. "When," she asked, "do we leave for New England?"

"In an hour, perhaps in two. As soon as I hear that our forces have consolidated their position in New England. Prepare yourself. You will leave separately. Segurius will go with you. He will—er—guard you. Now go!"

Zara turned and left the room. Outside, Segurius and Leon were standing in the hallway. Segurius, still in his vest and khaki trousers, loomed like a giant beside the puny Leon.

The big man stepped forward eagerly, asking Zara, "Well? What becomes of the girl?"

Zara smiled. "She will be released, my poor Segurius. She is to be returned to her Operator 5—provided the notebook is delivered according to the Master's instructions."

The massive face of Segurius contracted in a frown. He mumbled something under his breath, as he started for the door of the private room. Zara watched him, with an enigmatic look on her face. But Leon laid a hand on the big man's hairy arm.

"Wait, Segurius!" he whispered urgently. "You are wrought up. Be careful what you say to the Master."

Segurius pushed him roughly aside, flung open the door and strode into the room. The door slammed behind him, leaving Zara and Leon outside in the dimly lit hall.

Leon shook his head. "Segurius is not a proper disciple of the Master," he said. "He is too hot-headed. He puts himself and his pleasure above the good of the Cause."

Zara glanced keenly at the sincere, fanatical face of the little man. Suddenly she burst out laughing in a shrill, almost hysterical voice.

Leon looked at her, puzzled.

She stopped laughing abruptly. "The Cause!" she exclaimed acidly. "The Cause—you fool!"

Leon was shocked, stammering, "W-why, Zara—w-what do you mean?"

She leaned close to him, asked tensely:

"Have you ever seen the Master, Leon?"

"N-no. But I have heard him speak." The little man's face was suddenly lit up with a glow of fanatical ecstasy. "And his words brought the light to me! It is a Cause for which a man can willingly die!"

Zara shuddered. "Yes," she said, musingly. "When he talks he can make you feel that way. But if you ever saw him!" With a quick gesture of revulsion, she placed both hands before her face, whispering, "God grant that the Master be kinder to you than he was to me! God grant that he never lets you—see him!"

WITHIN THE room, Segurius was standing, his huge body hunched forward, his eyes burning hotly into the glare of the lamps.

From behind the desk came the cold voice of the Master: "What do you want, Segurius?"

"That girl, Master—the one whom I brought here. Zara tells me you are going to let her go. Master, I want that girl. Her face is beautiful, and there is a sweet smell about her. Master, do not let her go. Let me take her along when we leave here!"

"No, Segurius!"

The big man took a step closer to the desk. He was almost snarling. "I have served you faithfully, have I not? You promised me that I could have whatever I asked for when we become rulers of this land. Well, I want that girl!"

"No." The one word rapped out like the whip of a lash.

And Segurius, blinded with sudden rage, leaped swiftly toward the desk, his two big, gnarled hands reaching out toward the dim figure that sat behind the desk.

He snarled, "Then I kill you! My hands are strong. Even you—"

Abruptly the two lights went out. The single dim bulb of the desk burst into a dull glow. And Segurius saw the thing his hands were reaching for.

His whole body seemed to contract. His hands jerked back as if drawn by some mighty cord. A strangled cry sounded in his throat, and he pushed away from the desk, his face contorted with dread.

As quickly as they had gone out, the two flood lights snapped on again, and the desk lamp went off. The cool, mocking voice from behind the desk said, "Well, Segurius, you looked as if you wanted to throttle me. Why don't you?"

Once more that strangled cry sounded in the big man's throat, and he turned, pushed blindly from the room, hurried past Leon in the hallway without seeing him.

Leon looked after him, perplexed, then knocked on the door and entered. He blinked in the light and said, "Segurius is very angry about the girl, Master. He has been very useful to you. Perhaps—?"

The Master broke in curtly: "Segurius will give us no trouble, Leon. And I am releasing the girl for another purpose. It suits my needs to leave her here. So say no more about it. When that notebook is returned, let me know. I will talk to the girl once more, and then we shall let her go free."

"The notebook has been returned, Master. Our men took it from the boy at Fourteenth Street. The army truck which our men stole yesterday served a good purpose. They had to kill four policemen to escape. It seems that a trap was set, Master."

"So? And what happened?"

"Our car got away, Master, and the boy clung to the back of it. Our men pretended they did not know he was there. They drove here and came in through the private garage in the next street. They caught the boy and are holding him downstairs. What do you wish done with him, Master?"

"That is the same boy who caused all the trouble at headquarters number two, is it not, Leon?"

"Yes, Master."

"I think, Leon—" the voice behind the desk was cold, merciless "—that we will take that boy along with us. When we are established in New England, we will have a little—sport with him. Eh?"

CHAPTER 6
DOOM FROM THE AIR

G RAY DAWN streaked the east while a strange meeting took place in the Port Authority Building. A gray-haired man in the uniform of a major-general of the United States army stood behind a desk, spoke to the dozen or so men seated about the room. The face of the speaker was lined with care, and there were dark circles of worry under his eyes. His shoulders sagged as if from immense weariness. This man was Major-General Falk, Chief of Staff, who had flown from Washington to take charge of the situation.

A person intimate with diplomatic circles might have recognized many of those seated about the room—and might have wondered at the reason for their presence here in the offices of the United States Intelligence Service at this strange hour of the morning.

Among those men were the diplomatic attachés of the embassies of several European powers. The tall man with the white goatee and mustache, who sat near the door, was Count Peruga, of Italy. Close to him sat Sir Eric Bernard, of Great Britain. There were also representatives of France, Yugoslavia and Holland, as well as of several South American embassies.

In the back of the room stood Z-7, listening intently, with a worried frown, to the slowly spoken, deliberate words of Major-General Falk.

"Gentlemen," the General was saying, "you are all aware of the events which are taking place at this time." His gaze traveled from one to the other of the diplomatic representatives as he went on. "The United States is being invaded. You know that these strange rockets from hell, as the newspapers are calling them, have practically demolished all our coast defenses. And—" The General's tone became tense, bitter, "—we are forced to confess that we have not even been able to discover the identity of our invaders!

"Our Intelligence Service," General Falk continued bitterly, glancing in the direction of Z-7, "has been worse than useless. The best advice they could offer us was to meet the demands of this person who calls himself the Master of the Dragon. We have been forced to evacuate all of New England, and that territory, including the states of Maine, Vermont, New Hampshire and Rhode Island, is already in the hands of these invaders!"

A murmur of surprise and astonishment ran around the room. The news of the hasty evacuation and occupation of New England had been carefully kept from the press, and the announcement was startling news to these men.

"You have been summoned here," the Chief of Staff went on, "because one of our Secret Service operators has advanced certain theories. It was at this operator's suggestion that New England was evacuated. We have given him twelve hours in which to discover the secret of these rockets from hell. His time will be up at ten o'clock this morning. Until then, we are giving him every cooperation. In the interests of the safety of your own countries, gentlemen, I ask that you answer the questions that he will ask, as fully as you are able; for bear in mind that should these mysterious forces overrun this country, they would then be in a position to turn their attention to Europe and South America. And those rockets, gentlemen, will surely wreak the same havoc and destruction that they have spread in the United States!"

The gray-haired man ceased speaking, and a buzz of excited comment arose in the room.

General Falk wearily raised his hand and nodded to Z-7, who at once opened the door, saying to someone outside, "Has he come yet? All right. Tell him to come right in. We're waiting for him."

In a moment Jimmy Christopher entered the room. All eyes turned to him, but he glanced at none of them. His face was pale and drawn, his lips pressed tightly together into a thin line.

Z-7 asked him, low-voiced, "Any word of Diane or Tim, Jimmy?"

Operator 5 shook his head. He whispered, "I can't get a single clue, Chief. It's as if they'd both disappeared off the face of the earth. I—don't know where to look anymore!"

Z-7 placed a hand on his shoulder, pressing hard. "You've got to carry on, Jimmy. Keep a stiff upper lip."

Jimmy Christopher nodded, moved across the room. Now his glance met those of the assembled diplomats, and he bowed to many whom he knew. He made his way to the desk, shook hands with General Falk.

The Chief of Staff said to the seated men: "Gentlemen, this is Operator 5, of our Intelligence Service. I beg of you, answer his questions to the best of your ability."

Jimmy Christopher plunged directly into his topic, putting from his mind the thoughts of Diane and Tim that were gnawing at him.

"General Falk has no doubt outlined the situation to you. Thus far, no clue has presented itself as to the identity of the

Segurius jerked back as he saw the thing he was about to throttle!

invaders. We have received no news from the territory occupied by them, for the simple reason that they destroyed all means of communication as soon as they landed. We have not been receiving any radio broadcasts; it seems that they are silencing all stations as they advance. We have not heard from our agents who were planted in the occupied territory, and we can only assume that they have been apprehended, or that it has been made too dangerous for them to attempt to transmit a message."

As Jimmy paused for breath, Sir Eric Bernard stirred in his seat and said, "General Falk told us, Operator 5, that you have certain theories. May I ask what they are?"

"I am coming to that," Jimmy said crisply. He turned to the representative of Yugoslavia, who sat at the right of Sir Eric.

"Mr. Kovalescu," he said. "May I ask you a question?"

Kovalescu was a tall man, with a long, thin, sallow face. "Of course, Operator 5," he replied.

"In your country," Jimmy went on, "there was an organization shortly after the war, known as the Society of the Dragon, was there not?"

Kovalescu started slightly, snapped his fingers. "Surely there was!" he exclaimed. "But I never connected it with this Master of the Dragon—"

"Naturally not," Jimmy broke in, "after all these years. "It was an organization of terrorists, was it not?"

"That is so, as I recall," the Yugoslavian diplomat replied.

"And do you remember the name of the leader?"

The other men in the room were sitting tensely now, beginning to sense the drift of the question.

"I remember him distinctly, Operator 5, now that you bring the subject up. He was a Croatian by the name of Varniss, who had formerly been a professor of astronomical science at the University of Belgrade. He was an eloquent speaker, and he left his position at the University to lead an abortive uprising that almost made him the dictator of the Kingdom of the Serbs, Croats and Slovenes. But his *coup* failed, and he fled to Holland."

"Quite so," Jimmy said softly, his eyes shining. "Thank you, Mr. Kovalescu." He turned now to the representative of Holland.

"You, Mr. Van Zeeman," he said, "were attached to the staff of the governor of the Dutch East Indies some ten years ago, were you not?"

Van Zeeman, a small, portly man with a carefully trimmed mustache and Vandyke, nodded his head jerkily. His eyes showed admiration. "You are a very well-informed young man," he said. "It is true that I was the secretary to the Intendent—"

"Do you recall anything about a Croatian named Varniss who came to Java from Holland?"

"I do. That man was mad. He had a wild theory that he could construct a rocket to fly to the moon—*Lieber Gott!*—" Suddenly Van Zeeman broke off, his eyes widening as the full import of what he was saying struck home. *"A rocket!* It must be the same man!"

He glanced around at the others in the room. "My friends, I believe Operator 5 is on the right trail. These things connect!"

Sir Eric Bernard was frowning. "But there is no positive connection, don't you know, between this Varniss and the leader of the invaders of this country. It may all be coincidence. There are many things as yet unexplained. For instance—"

"Just a moment, Sir Eric," Jimmy interrupted. "I think we'll be able to establish the connection now. If you please, Mr. Van Zeeman, do you recall anything further about this Varniss?"

Van Zeeman appeared to meditate. "I recall that he actually had a model of a rocket, and of some sort of catapult to launch it. He was going to enclose himself in the rocket, and guide it by means of ailerons and a rudder. He had come to Java on a tramp steamer from Amsterdam, where he had got into some sort of trouble with the authorities. We were warned to look out for him, but he was very quiet in Java, working on his experiment. Shortly after that, he contracted leprosy, and we got permission of the United States Government to ship him off to Molokai Island, where there is a leper colony. I never heard of him since, but I remember him clearly. He was such a wild-eyed fellow, and so insistent that his rocket would work."

When Van Zeeman had finished, Jimmy exchanged a significant glance with Z-7, across the room. Then he said:

"Gentlemen, I can tell you what happened to Varniss after he was sent to Molokai. I have had the records in Washington searched, and I find that he escaped from the island almost a year ago!"

General Falk, standing beside Jimmy, stirred impatiently. "Do you mean to tell us, Operator 5, that this mad Croatian who escaped from a leper colony is the master of the forces who are invading the United States?"

"I do!" Jimmy Christopher said emphatically. "If you will have patience, gentlemen, I have just one or two more questions.

"Monsieur Sainte-Hilaire," he said, addressing the attaché of the French embassy, who sat directly opposite the desk. "The question I am about to ask you may prove embarrassing. But I hope that in the interests of world safety, you will answer it frankly."

Sainte-Hilaire allowed the smoke from his cigarette to trickle from his nostrils in a twin stream, then nodded. "I will do my best, young man."

"Will you tell us frankly," Jimmy asked, "whether the French government has experienced any difficulties recently in Guiana?"

The apparently innocent question caused the Frenchman to start visibly. He began to speak, hesitated. "No," he finally said, lowering his eyes.

Jimmy pressed him. "Monsieur Sainte-Hilaire, this is no time to keep secrets. The United States has called you all here, and is laying its cards on the table. Can you do less?"

Sainte-Hilaire raised his eyes, met the earnest ones of Jimmy Christopher. He turned his head to see that the gaze of every man in the room was upon him. At last he shrugged.

"I may be called home for speaking of this," he said, "for the Premier has enjoined utmost secrecy. But I will risk it." He paused, then went on quickly. "Yes. We have had trouble. In the penal colony at Guiana, there was an uprising of prisoners. Mysteriously, they were armed. Guards were killed. Half of the prisoners escaped on a strange ship that appeared in the harbor of Cayenne. Two thousand of the most depraved men in the world regained their liberty. They are at large today!"

Gasps of astonishment arose from the other diplomats. Excited questions were hurled at Sainte-Hilaire.

"Why did you keep this a secret from the rest of the world?" Sir Eric Bernard demanded fiercely.

"Because," the Frenchman responded, "it would have meant losing French Guiana. The United States would have invoked the Monroe Doctrine and ousted us from South America—deservedly—for we should have maintained adequate precautions against such a wholesale escape. We would have resisted, and the incident might have led to another world war. Therefore the Premier of France instructed me to keep the matter a secret. We have been searching for three months for those escaped felons—to no avail!"

As the buzz of excitement died away, Jimmy pressed his questions relentlessly. He was weaving for himself and for these men a complete pattern of events, which held the key to the identity of the invaders who were even now in possession of four New England states.

He raised his hand for silence. "One more thing. These men of the Dragon Society reached our shores in ships. Surely they did not build them. They must have taken them by force. Have you gentlemen received word from your governments of the disappearance of any steamships within the last three months?"

The representatives of Brazil, Argentina and Peru nodded violently. Señor Gothman, of Argentina, answered for them.

"Several steamers of the Pan-Pacific Line, which sailed from

Valparaiso and Santiago more than a month ago, are long over-due at their ports of destination. I have been queried by the Minister of Maritime Affairs, but have been able to report nothing. Those steamers carried no wireless. It is possible that they could have been boarded—"

Sir Eric Bernard interrupted. "If you will pardon me, Señor Gothman, I can report the same experience. Three ships of the British and Dominions Line have also been reported missing to Lloyd's of London."

Several other men chimed in to report steamers that had never reached their destinations within the past month.

Jimmy Christopher nodded somberly, glancing at Z-7 at the door, then turning to General Falk. "There, sir," he said to the Chief of Staff, "you have the whole picture. This man, Gregory Varniss, has recruited a band of desperate criminals, and has welded them into an army. He has provided them with ships. By his wonderful gift of oratory, he has managed also to convert numerous dupes who have been aiding him, by preaching peace and at the same time acting as saboteurs here in America. With this rocket which he has developed, he has destroyed our defense and is invading the United States. I do not doubt that his goal is a world empire!"

General Falk stared at Jimmy. "It is—unbelievable! No one man could accomplish all that—"

Operator 5 smiled. "Men have come close to mastering the world before, General, who started with less. Alexander had no rockets; neither did Xerxes. Napoleon started as a poor Corsican boy, with even less equipment than Varniss—"

"Yes, yes!" Falk exclaimed. "But this is the twentieth century. Things like that can't happen—"

"Nevertheless," Jimmy said softly, "New England is in the hands of invaders. A vast slice of our country has been cut off—"

Sir Eric Bernard arose from his seat. "What do you propose to do?" he asked. "Britain will cooperate in every way—if these invaders are allowed to consolidate in New England, they may turn their rockets upon Canada!"

General Falk brought his fist down on the desk with a resounding *thwack*.

"I'll tell you what we propose to do, Sir Eric!" He glared at Jimmy Christopher, then went on. "We are through with this cowardly business of retreating. At ten o'clock, the full forces of the United States will be thrown against these dragon men, or whoever they are. I have troops pouring into New York and Connecticut. Mines are being delivered to the Navy Yard, to be laid along the coast and along all the roads by which the enemy could advance from New England. Planes have already been ordered up, to reconnoiter the enemy position. It is unthinkable that a small force of depraved men under a leprous leader should be able to intimidate and conquer a whole—"

Suddenly his voice died away as there came, through the open windows, the sound of that weird whistling from the sky. The faces of the men in the room blanched.

"Another rocket!"

Jimmy pushed across the room to a window, and the others crowded behind him. The early morning was gray and rainy. The screaming whistle sounded somewhere to the south, and there, high in the heavens, they perceived a comet-like object cleaving through the sky. One moment it was visible breaking through the mist, giving off fiery sparks as its tremendous speed cut the air. Then it suddenly headed downward.

A sigh went up as those in the room realized that it was not headed in their direction, but was descending at a point somewhere in Brooklyn. The time between that realization and the explosion which followed was infinitesimal. Suddenly the earth seemed to rock, the building shook. The crashing thunder of the explosion, perhaps five miles away, almost deafened them. Panes of glass from the window shattered in their faces.

From their high position in the Port Authority Building, they could see for miles, across the bay, and into Brooklyn. Jimmy Christopher saw a huge geyser of flame shoot high into the air at the point where the rocket had struck. Burst upon burst of minor explosions followed the first terrific holocaust, and the morning mists were cut by red blasts of flame.

General Falk exclaimed in a hushed voice, "My God! Where did that strike?"

Jimmy Christopher turned to him somberly. "That, General," he said very low, "was the Brooklyn Navy Yard! There go all your mines!"

The white faces of the other men shone, reflected in the glow of the distant fires. Falk slumped into a chair, shoulders sagging. He looked like a beaten man.

The clangor of fire apparatus sounded from the streets below them. Engines were already rushing from all parts of the city to the stricken area. Jimmy knew that there was no hope whatever of salvaging any part of the Navy Yard. The apparatus could, at least, prevent the fire from spreading through the rest of Brooklyn.

Jimmy turned away from the window, was about to address the Chief of Staff, when the phone on the desk rang. Z-7 picked it up, listened and extended the instrument to General Falk. "For you, sir," he said.

While the foreign diplomats huddled together near the window, talking in low tones, General Falk answered the phone. After a moment he put it down, gazed about the room like a hunted animal.

"That was Captain Loring, calling from Mitchell Field," he told Jimmy and Z-7 in a low voice so that the others could not hear. "He was the commander of the air squadron that I sent up to reconnoiter. His whole squadron was destroyed by anti-aircraft guns, and he alone escaped. He reports that the enemy have spread out from the coast of Maine, using Fort Wetherill in Rhode Island as their base. He is sure that the rocket which destroyed the Navy Yard came from Wetherill. He says that the enemy have built something that looks like a catapult on the battlements. He did not have a good chance to observe it, for he had all he could do to dodge the anti-aircraft barrage."

"In that case," said Z-7, "it should be possible to bombard Wetherill with long range guns from New York. Once their catapult is destroyed—"

"That's it!" exclaimed General Falk, his eyes suddenly flashing. "I'll phone Hamilton and Niagara—"

His voice broke as a dull concussion shook the building. The reverberations of another terrific explosion tore through the room. The explosion sounded, to Jimmy Christopher, as if it had taken place within a few miles of them.

Falk gasped. "Another one! They—?"

Hard upon the heels of that explosion there sounded another, and another. The room seemed to be continually rocking. Flames lit the sky to the east and west as well as the south. Jimmy Christopher, looking out of the window, pointed and said to Z-7:

"See those flames, Chief? That looks like Governor's Island; and over there, beyond the flames of the Navy Yard—that's Staten Island—"

"Good God!" Z-7 said in a hushed voice. "That would be Fort Jay on Governor's, and Fort Wadsworth on Staten Island. They're not giving us a chance—"

Once more the phone rang, and Z-7 answered it. Hardly had he put it down, when it rang again. His dark eyes flashed, and his fingers drummed nervously on the glass top of the desk. The assembled diplomats were almost ready for his hoarse announcement:

"The rockets have destroyed every fort in New York! Schuyler, Slocum, Wood, Wadsworth—every one! They've beaten us to the punch. They're not leaving a single big gun with which we can fight them!"

General Falk squared his shoulders. He arose, faced Jimmy Christopher. "Operator 5, your policy of non-resistance is proving no good. While we knuckle under, they are rendering us absolutely helpless. I am not going to wait any longer!" He reached for the telephone. "I shall order a general advance. I have two full divisions concentrated in New York and New Jersey. I shall throw them against the enemy. I shall order every plane available into the air. We will roll over these desperadoes like a cloud of—"

Jimmy Christopher seized Falk's arm just as he was lifting the receiver off.

"You mustn't do that, General!" he exclaimed. "A single rocket landing in the midst of marching men will destroy an entire regiment. You have seen the power of the explosive in those rockets. I have a better plan, General."

Falk shook off his hand. "Bah! We should never have listened to you in the first place. You, and that boy of yours. If he hadn't betrayed us by returning that notebook, we might have been prepared for this. We might have had it decoded by now, and known of their plans. We could at least have saved the men who perished in those forts!"

Jimmy Christopher stepped back, lowered his head. He had no answer to make to that argument by the general.

Slowly, he turned and started for the door. Z-7, looking after him with a worried gaze, pushed through the press of diplomats who had watched the scene with avid interest. He caught up with Operator 5 at the door.

"Where are you going, Jimmy?" His voice was full of concern. He had worked together with Operator 5 for so many years that he had grown to love the young man almost as a son. "For God's sake, Jimmy, don't do anything rash."

Jimmy Christopher laughed harshly. "Rash! What difference

does it make what happens to me? I'm not wanted here. Diane and Tim are gone!" Suddenly he turned, pushed out of the room.

Z-7 gazed after him, took a step to follow, then stopped as Falk called out: "Let that young fool go, Z-7. Come here. I have work for you."

Z-7 turned back toward the desk with a heavy heart. General Falk was rapping commands into the phone, while flames from a dozen points in the city put the bleak dawn to shame....

CHAPTER 7
SUICIDE LEGION

JIMMY CHRISTOPHER, when he left the room, did not at once depart from the offices of Intelligence headquarters. He stopped at one of the phone booths provided for the use of agents and phoned Mitchell Field, to ask whether Captain Loring was still there.

In a moment he was talking to the flight commander, who had just returned alone from the reconnoitering expedition into New England. He knew Captain Loring, and was known to the aviator. Jimmy had made use of the captain's services in the past.

"This is Operator 5," he said. "Is your plane in condition to take off at once for another flight into New England, Captain?"

"I've just finished checking it over," Loring told him. "Aside from a few bullet holes in the wings, it's in tiptop shape. What's in the wind?"

"I'm coming out there," Jimmy replied. "I'll want you to take me into New England, as near to Wetherill as possible, and land me there. It'll be dangerous—"

"You know I don't mind the danger," Loring broke in. "But," he added doubtfully, "General Falk told me on the phone to await his instructions. Are you acting under the general's orders?"

For a second Jimmy hesitated. Then he said truthfully, "I've just come from talking to the general. I was there when you phoned."

"All right, then," Loring said. "I just didn't want to disobey the general. But as long as you talked to him—"

"I'm starting at once," Jimmy interrupted hurriedly. "See you soon, old man."

He left the booth, his keen blue eyes reflecting the spirit of the daring plan he had conceived on the spur of the moment. But he had not taken three steps before the clerk on duty at the switchboard in the outer office called to him:

"Operator 5! Call for you. It's the police department!"

Jimmy frowned, said, "I'll take it in the booth." He hurried back, lifted the receiver, and suddenly felt warm blood racing through his veins as a voice came to him over the phone:

"Sergeant Mulvaney speaking, Precinct four-fifteen. We've got a girl here who gives her name as Diane Elliot. Patrolman Schultz found her wandering near the East River. She insisted we call you. You know her?"

"Do I know her!" Jimmy exclaimed. "Hold everything. I'll be right over!"

He hung up, phoned Mitchell Field and left word for Loring

84

that he would be a little delayed, and fairly raced from the offices, punching the button until an elevator arrived to take him down.

Outside he hailed a cab and barked, "Precinct four-fifteen!"

On the way across town, the cabby had to detour twice to avoid long silent columns of marching men in khaki. They were contingents of the regular army, moving northward; the first of the forces which Falk was flinging against the invaders in New England. There were also companies of mechanized infantry, and gun corps. At Fifth Avenue they had to wait ten minutes while a contingent of Miners and Sappers marched past. All these men wore grim, tight expressions....

THEY COULD see the flames from the Navy Yard still raging; the fires that marked the spots where Forts Jay and Wadsworth had stood only a short hour ago. And far to the north, they could see more flames—the funeral pyres of the garrisons of Slocum and Schuyler. The soldiers knew that they were marching to a similar doom; a doom that would be preceded for a fraction of a second by the sinister, weird whistling in the sky, followed by a cataclysmic explosion that would hurl their bleeding, broken bodies into the air, or pound them horridly into the earth.

They knew that this doom awaited them, yet they marched stoically northward. Jimmy's eyes clouded. His own plan was suicidal, yet if it succeeded, all these men might still be spared for their families.

Due to the interruptions and detours, it was more than twenty-five minutes before Jimmy Christopher reached the police precinct-house.

He ordered the cabby to wait, lunged into the station house. "Miss Elliot," he demanded of the sergeant at the desk. "Where is she?"

The sergeant threw him a queer look, got up and came around in front. "Follow me, sir," he said.

He led Jimmy across the floor into the captain's room. "The captain is out now," he explained, "so I figured I'd let her wait in there."

He pushed the door open, stood aside for Jimmy to enter. Operator 5 pushed past him into the small office, his eyes fixed on Diane, who stood in the far corner, staring at him.

If he had wondered on the way over why Diane had been picked up by a policeman—why she was waiting for him in a station house instead of having come directly back—those questions passed from his mind and gave way to graver ones as he saw the change that a few hours had wrought in the beautiful, chestnut-haired girl.

Now her cheeks were gaunt, and there was no color in them. Though nothing could detract from the trimness of her figure, her smartly tailored sports suit was rumpled now, disheveled. Her eyes were wide open and seemed to have lost their usual keen clarity. One who did not know her as well as Jimmy did might almost have thought that she was not the same person.

But Jimmy Christopher knew that she must have undergone some dreadful experience in the last few hours. She looked almost—he was afraid to think it—as if some unbearable shock had been inflicted on her mind.

"Diane!" he exclaimed in quick sympathy. He pushed the door

closed, shutting out the gaze of the curious sergeant, and strode across the room to her, his arms extended in warm greeting.

And Diane Elliot shrank away from Jimmy Christopher!

EARLIER THAT morning, a huge, black cabin-plane had taken off from a private landing field on Long Island and swung its ebon snout northeastward. Within that cabin, behind the pilot's compartment, sat three people—the beautiful, dark-eyed Zara, the small Leon, and, behind them, a man in a long cloak, whose face and head were entirely covered by a black hood which, on close inspection, could be seen to be made of leather. His hands also, were encased in black leather gauntlets.

This man sat motionless, silent, staring out the window at the swiftly speeding panorama below. In the forward seats, Leon and Zara fidgeted.

The woman wore a black raincoat, but no hat. The raincoat was open at the throat, and Leon cast sidelong, admiring glances at her regal beauty.

Abruptly, the black-clothed man in the rear stirred and broke the silence. "You are sure, Leon," he asked, "that Segurius followed the girl?"

Leon twisted in his seat, faced backward. "Yes, Master. I saw him turn the corner after her, when we dropped her from the car near the East River. We were going the other way. By the time we had turned the car around and got back to the corner, we saw a policeman talking to the girl, and of Segurius there was no sign. We remained and watched to be sure that she was taken to the station-house, where Segurius could not follow, and then we returned."

The Master grunted. "I misjudged Segurius. I thought that his devotion to the Cause was greater than any other passion with him." He shrugged. "But it doesn't matter. Segurius and those others who talked on the street corners have served their purpose. Now that there is martial law in all the cities, they could no longer conduct peace meetings anyway." He chuckled. "They were useful, those peace meetings. They gained us many recruits for the rockets. Segurius would have made a good recruit for a rocket."

Zara shuddered, not turning to look at the black-hooded man.

He noted the shiver that coursed down her frame, said to her, "What is it, my dear Zara? Is it that you find me too—cold-blooded? Remember that a man who is destined to rule the world must not have human emotions!"

She turned a tortured face to him. "Then why do you keep me with you always?" she cried. "Why must you—?"

She stopped, as if she realized the futility of going further, as if it were a protest that she had often repeated and to which she knew the answer.

The Master laughed mockingly. "You, my dear Zara," he said, "are my only weakness. From the moment that I saw you in that theater in Belgrade, I knew that I would one day make you the empress of the world!" His voice grew lower, assumed an edge of cruelty that seemed to cut through Zara like a knife.

"And I preserve you, beautiful one, for the day when I shall hand you up to the seat beside my throne. Some day, though, I shall give myself the pleasure of—touching you, my dear Zara;

90

of fondling your beautiful body. After that you will lose your beauty. Your skin will turn—"

"Stop! Stop!" she suddenly screamed. "Stop!" She covered her face with her hands, and a tremor wracked her.

Leon looked on deprecatingly, while the Master's chuckle sounded again.

"Where is that boy, Leon?" the hooded man asked. "I hope you did not lose him the way you lost Segurius?"

"No, Master. I made sure that he left by the first plane. He will be at the fort—awaiting your pleasure."

AT THAT moment the plane banked and began to descend. Looking over the side, the three passengers could see the gloomy shape of Fort Wetherill. To the east was the broad expanse of the Atlantic, and all along the coast there were heaps of smoldering ruins that had been other fortifications. Wetherill was the only one spared by the rockets—evidently because the invaders had planned to use it.

The plane taxied to a landing in a field under the shadow of the fort. There were other planes here, and a general air of bustling activity. Grim, hard-faced men in blue uniforms and Sam Browne belts hurried about the fort. At one point, a peculiar-looking device projected from the wall. It resembled a huge lathe, with two steel rails that pointed up into the air at an angle of perhaps fifty degrees. On the field, and at various places on the fort, long anti-aircraft guns pointed their muzzles at the skies.

A company of blue-uniformed men stood at attention beside the plane while the hooded man alighted with Zara and Leon. The officer in charge of the company saluted stiffly, then raised his hand in a signal. The big guns of the fort thundered out a salute, firing salvo after salvo. It was an imperial welcome, and the hooded man seemed pleased, for he rubbed his hands together.

When the thunder of the guns died away, the officer approached, bowing low.

"You are most welcome, Master," he said. "Everything is prepared for you. Our operations have met with complete success."

He spoke in English, but there was a marked, guttural accent, similar to that of the Master. The Master's voice, coming from behind the hood, sparkled with satisfaction.

"You have done well, Komroff. As a reward, I hereby name you generalissimo of all the forces of the new Empire of the Dragon. And when we have spread our conquest to the rest of the world, you shall be the Viceroy of America!"

Komroff bowed low.

Behind the Master, Zara's eyes burned into his back with a loathing and hatred which it was well that he did not see....

"And now," said the Master, "let us raise our flag on the first territory to yield to the Dragon Empire!"

Komroff saluted, swiveled in smart military style, and barked a command to a junior officer, who in turn passed it on to the company of soldiers. Once more they came to attention. A drummer beat a strange tattoo on a drum, and at once all activity ceased on the field. Men stopped walking, and stood still. Mechanics left the planes they were working on, and stood stiffly at attention.

And slowly, a flag arose on the flagstaff atop Fort Wetherill—a flag that in no way resembled the Stars and Stripes; a flag which bore upon its black background the scarlet figure of a coiled dragon—the symbol of the Dragon Empire.

The Master now crossed the field slowly and entered the fort. Close behind him followed Zara, and Leon, and the newly created General Komroff.

Komroff was a stocky man, with a wide-spreading walrus mustache that might have made anyone else look ridiculous but only added to the awesomeness of his appearance. He twirled the ends of that mustache now, as he threw glances of admiration at the svelte figure of Zara. Leon saw those glances, and his teeth showed in a snarl which vanished at once, as Komroff turned his gaze upon the little man.

Zara, for her part, seemed unaware of the admiration of the general. She walked behind the Master, her beautiful head held high, her eyes still on the hooded man's back.

WITHIN THE castle, the huge assembly hall had been converted into a throne room. At one end, a high dais had been erected, and upon it had been placed a heavy gilded armchair.

The Master seated himself on the improvised throne, and motioned for Zara to take her place on his left and for Leon to stand at his right.

Then he said to Komroff, "You have no difficulty with discipline?"

Komroff grinned, showing black, uneven, discolored teeth. "None, Master. These jailbirds have been used to harsher discipline in the penal colony. Here they are in paradise. A few had to be shot at first, as examples. Now there is no trouble whatever. You saw how well they paraded just now."

The hooded man nodded, drumming with his gloved fingers on the edge of the chair. The eyes that peered out from the two slits in the hood seemed to be drinking in the great hall, with dragon flags draped along the walls, with the dozen guards at the various doors, in attitudes of rigid attention. The Master appeared to be drunk with power.

Komroff said, "If you please, Master, the recruits for the rockets whom you sent up here seem to be losing a little of their enthusiasm for suicide. Perhaps you should talk to them again."

The Master turned his hooded face toward Komroff, as if unwillingly bringing himself back from his thoughts of glory. "So!" he snapped. "Their zeal is wearing off? What do you think, Leon? Should I speak to them again?"

Leon seemed to consider. "We shall need them, Master. There are more rockets to be launched. Perhaps you should."

"Very well," said the hooded man. "Have them brought in."

While Komroff went to the door to issue orders, the Master said to Zara, "Well, my dear, how does the thought of being my empress appeal to you now?"

She lowered her eyes before his gaze. "I—don't—know," she replied in a choked voice.

Before the Master could say anything further, Komroff returned. As he walked across the room, his gaze seemed to be centered in a fascinated stare upon Zara. He withdrew his eyes from her reluctantly, and said to the hooded man: "The Suicide Legion comes now, Master."

Outside, in the hall, there sounded the tread of marching feet, and a strange company deployed into the room. There were perhaps forty of them, young men and old, dressed in civilian clothing, but each wearing a red scarf on his right sleeve. They marched into the room in a column of fours, following a thin, ascetic old man who acted as their leader.

They halted facing the throne in a double line, and at a signal from the old man they all raised their voices in chorus and chanted:

"Master, we, who are about to die, salute you!"

As they chanted, they raised their right arms before them in a gesture similar to the Fascist salute. The loud, clear voices rang through the room in a manner that caused a tingle to course through the blood of the woman, Zara. To her, that strangely chanted salute was reminiscent of the words spoken two thousand years ago by the legions of Rome as they were reviewed by Julius Caesar before going into battle: *"Caesar, te morituri salutamus!"*

Those Roman legionaries had gone to their death with those words on their lips; and now, two thousand years later, a group of fanatics uttered the counterpart of those words.

And just as Julius Caesar must have responded, so did the hooded man. He arose from his gilded chair, raised his right hand, and began to speak. A hush fell upon the room as the voice came from behind that strange black hood.

SUBTLY, THE voice seemed to have changed. It was no longer guttural, tinged with a hint of cruelty. It was a honeyed, silver voice, which persuaded, cajoled, flattered, promised, by turns. It was the voice of a great orator; of one who could sway men, could lead them in a lost cause. Such a man could be a tremendous force for good; but he could be an even greater force for evil.

As he spoke, he seemed to weave a spell about those in the room, even including Zara.

"You are men," he intoned, "who have devoted your lives to the great Cause of Peace. I have told you before that peace can only come through pain and suffering. Like a surgeon who ruthlessly cuts away a cancerous growth, we are cutting away from this earth the paraphernalia and the implements of warfare. Soon, the benighted people of this land shall live in peace—for we are destroying their armaments and their forts, their guns and their ships. We shall go on, until there is no more will to war upon the earth. Then all men shall live in tranquility and in happiness. You and I, my friends, will be dead on that day, but our task will have been well done, and our names shall go down through the centuries."

He paused, watched the effect of his words upon the Suicide Legion, then went on: "Lest it be said that I seek personal glory from this great undertaking, I cover my face with this hood. And I give you my solemn oath that when our work is done, I, too, shall follow you into death. Already, fifteen of your number have gone into glorious eternity, guiding our rockets to the mark. Soon you shall be called upon to take your places in the rockets. Will you be ready?"

A great shout came from the throats of the forty of the Suicide Legion: "Master, we are ready!"

"Then go to your quarters, and await the word!"

Their leader snapped a command, and they swung into a column of fours again. At another signal they broke into the same chant they had uttered upon entering, but this time with greater enthusiasm: "Master, we, who are about to die, salute you!"

And they marched out of the room.

Komroff watched them until they had disappeared and the heavy tread of their feet had faded down the hall. Then his thick lips twisted into a grim smile under his wide mustache.

"Master," he said sardonically, "I, who am not about to die, salute you! You are the greatest orator the world has ever seen. I cannot understand how you can work these men up to the point where they are ready to sacrifice their lives for a cause which does not even exist!"

The hooded man chuckled. "A matter of salesmanship, Komroff," he said dryly. "And now, bring in that boy with the freckles. We will see if we cannot—er—convert him, too!"

CHAPTER 8
THE GIFT OF DEATH

JIMMY CHRISTOPHER faced Diane Elliot in the captain's office of the precinct house. His eyes expressed puzzlement and hurt as the glad welcome he had uttered died on his lips.

Diane shrank back against the wall, seeming to try to get as far away from him as she could. And she gasped hoarsely, "Don't touch me!"

Jimmy stopped less than a foot from her. "Diane!" he rasped. "What is it? Why—?"

He put his hand out again, wishing to caress her, to comfort her, but she screamed again, "Don't, Jimmy! Don't touch me!"

He saw agony reflected in her features—agony of mind. Her eyes were opened wide, as if she were seeing some horrid picture that she couldn't get rid of. Her breasts were heaving spasmodically, and her little hands were clenched at her sides.

"Jimmy!" she moaned. "Will you do something for me?"

"Of course, Diane. Anything you say."

"Please, Jimmy, have me put in a cell, in jail. Have me locked up today!"

"Locked up?" he echoed "But why?"

"I—I'm afraid—of myself!"

Jimmy Christopher stared at her silently, trying to understand the thing that had come over her. His mouth tightened. "That man did something to you. Tell me quickly, Diane."

She closed her eyes. "He—he let me look at him. And then he talked to me. He gave me orders!"

"He gave you orders?" Jimmy repeated without understanding.

"Orders!" Suddenly she started to laugh, half-hysterically. "Do you know what orders he gave me? I am going to help him destroy—"

With a swift, desperate motion she turned her back to Jimmy

Christopher, faced the wall. "No, no! I mustn't tell you. You'd never let me do it!"

Operator 5 stepped close to her, put both hands on her shoulders, and swung her around, facing him. He took her quivering body in his arms, holding her tight. "You must tell me, Diane," he said very low.

Suddenly deep sobs wracked her body, and she rested her head on his shoulder. Jimmy stroked her hair, let her cry. His mind was working swiftly, trying to fathom the reason for Diane's queer actions, for her strange words.

She moaned, "Jimmy! I—I was afraid of this. I—I was afraid that if you took me in your arms like this, I—I wouldn't be able to resist telling you everything. And then—then—you'd never let me do it. Promise me, Jimmy, that you'll let me do what I have to!"

HE LED her to the chair behind the captain's desk, seated her in it gently, and stood before her. "I can't promise, Diane," he said softly. "Because I think I know what it is you have been ordered to do."

She raised her head quickly, alarmed. "You—know?"

"Let me see. Has it something to do with Tim?"

She started, exclaimed: "You *do* know, Jimmy! How—how did you guess?"

He shrugged. "I know you feel about Tim the way I do. I'm almost sure they must have gotten hold of Tim again, otherwise he'd have turned up. Did he order you to do something for him in order to save Tim's life?"

She nodded, gazing up at him breathlessly. "That man—that Master of theirs—is a—a—"

"Leper!" Jimmy finished for her.

"Yes!" she whispered. "You know that, too?"

"I just found it out."

"He is, Jimmy, he is. He—he let me look at his face. Oh, God!"

She bent her head, covered her own face. "It—it was—terrible. And he's taking Tim along with him—to New England. He's left already, by plane. And—and he's going to—to *touch Tim;* to make a leper of Tim! And I can save him, Jimmy!"

"What does he want you to do?"

"Those rockets—they're guided by men—living men, who are willing to give up their lives for the Master. The man in the rocket follows a radio beam. And I—I'm supposed to get into Intelligence headquarters, and set the beam going. He gave me this—" She took from her handbag a small, black box with a key similar to a telegraph key at the top of it. At the side of the box was a plug to fit into a socket. "This box sends out the beam. I'm supposed to plug it into an outlet in headquarters, and start it working. If I do that, and the rocket reaches its destination, Tim will be spared!"

Jimmy Christopher's eyes clouded, and little ridges showed along his jaw muscles as he took the box from her. "And you were going to do this, Diane?"

"I don't know what I was going to do. I think I would have done it—without telling you. How can I leave Tim to such a fate? Can't we warn them in headquarters, and have everyone leave before I plug the box in?"

Jimmy thought swiftly. "What time were you told to do this?"

"The rocket will be started at seven o'clock tonight. I'm to set the beam at any time before that."

Jimmy nodded. "That'll give us plenty of time for what I want to do. Come along, Diane."

He took her hand, literally dragged her out of the room, through the station house and into the street.

She gasped, "W-where are you taking me, Jimmy?"

Operator 5 bundled her into the taxi-cab, gave an address to the driver.

"We're going to Dad's house," he told her. "I'm going to have Dad take care of you and see that you don't get into trouble, while I attend to a little business."

The street number which he had given to the cabby was the location of the house known in the records of United States Intelligence as "Address Y." It was the home of John Christopher, Jimmy's father, formerly known as Q-6 in the Secret Service. John Christopher was retired now, due to wounds received in the performance of his duty. But he was not past lending a hand on occasion, when Jimmy or the service needed him, and Operator 5 had practically made the home of his father his own headquarters.

AS THE cab pulled away from in front of the station house, daylight had come to the city. But it was day that was full of misery and peril and sadness for the populace. As if forming a great ring about the city, smoking piles to the east, west, south and north indicated the spots where the rockets from hell had laid low the great forts erected for defense.

Marching soldiers and rumbling trucks were everywhere. And the few civilians who were in the streets walked with a furtive nervousness, as if expecting every moment that another rocket would whistle its litany of death through the skies.

Within the cab, Diane was begging:

"Jimmy! You're going into danger! Take me along. I can't stand staying behind, knowing what will happen to Tim."

Jimmy Christopher stared straight ahead, bleak-eyed. "Dad will take care of you, Di. And where I'm going—I can't take you!"

Had Jimmy Christopher looked behind, he would have seen the small coupé which persistently followed the cab at a discreet distance. But he was so occupied with his own bitter thoughts that he did not see the coupé, or the man who was driving it.

That man was Segurius. And his hot, mad eyes never left the cab as he kept after it till it reached Address Y. He drove past the house while Jimmy and Diane were entering, and parked at the corner. Then he turned in the seat and kept watch on the entrance through which they had disappeared.

Inside, John Christopher gravely greeted his son and Diane. His keen intuition immediately told him that both were under some sort of high tension, and he led them into the sitting room, prepared some tea for them. While he was brewing it on the electric stove in the corner, Jimmy examined the oblong box that Diane had given him.

"Did you ever see anything like this, Dad?" he asked.

John Christopher glanced toward it, frowned. "No. What is it?"

Diane, who had been sitting on the edge of her chair, said,

"It's supposed to send out a radio beam to guide a rocket." She took it from Jimmy's hand, walked over to the corner where the stove was. She spoke tensely: "Dad, if I don't plug this into an outlet in Intelligence headquarters before seven o'clock tonight, Tim Donovan will become a leper!"

John Christopher's somber eyes regarded her, then the box.

"Tell me about it," he said simply. He poured the tea, placed it upon a serving table and wheeled it to the couch. When they were seated and sipping the hot beverage, Diane told him the whole story. Jimmy didn't appear to be listening. His brow was corrugated in thought.

Diane finished her story, her cheeks flushed with excitement. "So you see, Dad, why this Master of theirs let me go? I've got to set the box to guide his rocket."

John Christopher looked at his son. "What are you going to do, Jimmy?"

Jimmy Christopher arose abruptly, paced up and down. "I've got an army plane waiting at Mitchell Field. I'm going to have the pilot land me in New England, somewhere, as close to Fort Wetherill as possible. I'm going to try to get into one of those rockets, *and guide it back against Wetherill!*"

THEY BOTH gazed at him in a hushed silence. Then John Christopher said huskily, "You're going to—sacrifice your life, son?"

Diane sprang up, seized his arm. "No, Jimmy. There must be some other way. You can't deliberately throw away your life—"

"Why not?" Jimmy asked fiercely. "I'm not letting you set that box, though it means Tim's death. I was ready to keep that notebook, even if it meant your life, Di. Shall I be more careful of my own life?"

John Christopher pushed back his chair, got up slowly. He stood facing his son, and their eyes met. "Let me go, Jimmy," Q-6 said softly. "I'm an old man. I've little left to live for. It would be a—glorious way to die!"

Jimmy Christopher shook his head stubbornly. "It's my idea, Dad—and it's my job!"

The older man glanced hopelessly at Diane. They both knew him well, knew the futility of arguing with Jimmy Christopher about a thing like this.

"And Tim?" Diane asked slowly. "If they've got Tim in Wetherill, he'll perish when the fort is destroyed."

"I know he will," Operator 5 said hoarsely. "And I hope he forgives me."

The three of them were silent. In their minds was a picture of young, freckle-faced Tim Donovan; of his infectious grin and his happy laughter.

"At that," Jimmy went on, "it'll be better than the thing that the Dragon Master plans for him."

Diane exclaimed impetuously, "Jimmy! Why can't I plug in this box? We can have them empty headquarters, and let the rocket strike—"

Jimmy smiled at her indulgently. He turned the box over in his hands. "Look, Di, I've been experimenting for more than a year with radio beams. Although you can't tell what science may develop, I'm reasonably certain that no radio beam could be caused to emanate from this little thing. This box isn't what you think it is!"

Her eyes opened wider. "You mean the Dragon Master was deceiving me?"

"Of course."

"Then why—?"

"Because this little box probably contains the same sort of powerful explosive that's used in the rockets. When you plug it in and depress the key, it'll probably send you as well as headquarters into kingdom come. Don't you see, Di, that the Dragon Master must have known that you'd tell me about this—that we'd look around for some way out of it, and that we'd probably try this box out to see how it worked?"

Understanding suddenly flashed in her eyes. "Then this—?"

"Is nothing more than a powerful bomb, if my guess is correct."

John Christopher nodded. "It was intended to eliminate Operator 5, whom the Dragon Master couldn't get at in any other way."

Operator 5 carefully put the box in his pocket. "Maybe," he said dreamily, "it will prove a boomerang!"

CHAPTER 9
ONE-MAN OFFENSIVE

WHEN JIMMY CHRISTOPHER departed from Address Y, some twenty minutes later, he left two people there with the almost certain knowledge that they would never see him again. At the door, he exchanged a long, silent handclasp with his father.

John Christopher gulped and said: "Good luck, Jimmy. I—"

He could speak no further, and turned, stumbling blindly into the house. Diane reached up, took Jimmy Christopher's head between her two hands, and kissed him on the lips. Her eyes were wet.

"Won't you at least let me go with you to the airport?" she asked.

He smiled. "No, Di. You'd manage somehow to go further." He crushed her to him for a single moment of ecstasy, then released her and hurried down the steps of the

Mitchell Field was blasted from the face of the earth!

106

stoop, went to the garage in the rear of the house. In a moment, he drove out in his big, Diesel-engine roadster, waved to her, and swung west.

Diane watched him till he turned the corner. She did not see Segurius in the coupé at the other corner, for in her eyes there was a stubborn resolve that translated itself into action.

The moment Jimmy's roadster had disappeared, she glanced back to see if John Christopher were near, then hastened down the steps to the sidewalk instead of returning into the house. She was clutching her handbag, and she ran toward the corner around which Jimmy's roadster had turned. Her intention was to hail a cab and drive to Mitchell Field. Somehow or other she was determined to get on board the plane with him. She hadn't taken her hat, and her chestnut hair streamed in the wind as she ran. She didn't see Segurius until he stepped from the coupé, almost in her path.

The sight of the huge man brought a startled cry to her lips. She swerved in her course, tried to dodge him.

But he reached out a hairy hand, seized her by the arm, and swung her into the coupé. She gasped, tried to get out, but his huge body blocked the way. He got in, gripped her two hands in one of his, holding her helpless, and got the car started with the other hand.

Thus far, neither of them had spoken. Segurius raced the car around the corner, then settled down to speed grimly northward. He released his grip on her, and Diane at once reached for the door to open it and leap out. She got it open, was halfway out, ready to jump from the speeding coupé, when Segurius gripped her by the shoulder, drew her in again.

"I mean you no harm," he said, reaching across her and slamming the door again. "It is that I wish you to be safe that I take you away with me. You are wrong to fear me."

She slumped in her seat, white-faced, desperate. She was no match for the man's sheer strength.

As he drove his eyes stole sideways greedily to drink in her fresh young beauty. His thick lips carved into a smile, and he said, "I have risked much for you, beautiful one. I have brought on my head the hatred of the Master. I could have been a prince of the new Empire of the Dragon, if I had gone with him. Instead, I stayed to be near you; now I take you to a place which I know of here in the city. We will live there happily—you and I! From the beginning of time, beautiful one, you were destined for me!"

Diane kept herself outwardly calm by a supreme exertion of will. She recognized that this man was in the grip of tremendous passion. It frightened her.

Suddenly Segurius uttered an oath. He was looking in the rear-vision mirror, and Diane turned to see what had alarmed him. She uttered a low, joyful cry.

Behind them, less than half a block away, she recognized the long, powerful roadster of Jimmy Christopher. By some miracle he had picked them up. Diane could not understand how, for he had headed south when he turned the corner. And now he was behind them, gaining swiftly.

Segurius' face was suffused with rage. He snarled, gripped the wheel in his powerful hands, and pressed the accelerator down to the floorboards. The coupé raced away, but the Diesel-engine roadster inexorably closed up the distance. Diane, still glancing behind, could see Jimmy Christopher's set, grim face behind the wheel.

THE COUPÉ swerved wildly from side to side as it gained speed under Segurius' down-pressed foot. At this early hour of the morning, there was little traffic and the street was clear as far ahead as they could see. The speedometer needle crept up to sixty, to seventy, to seventy-five. That seemed to be the coupé's limit of speed. Diane knew though, that the roadster behind them could do more than a hundred without effort. It was certain that Jimmy would catch up, but what would happen then? At this terrific rate, Jimmy Christopher would never dare to cut them off.

Two, three, four street corners flashed by. Now the roadster was abreast of them, now it was nosing ahead. Jimmy Christopher was staring across at them, slowly pulling ahead.

Segurius cursed, took his right hand from the wheel and dragged a heavy revolver from the waistband of his trousers. He rested its muzzle on his left forearm, aiming it at Jimmy through the open window. Jimmy Christopher made no effort to dodge. Instead, he swung his roadster a little closer.

In a moment, Segurius would fire. A shot striking anywhere would be fatal to Jimmy at this speed, marvelous driver though he was. Diane realized this, and just at the instant that Segurius contracted his finger on the trigger of his weapon, she reached down and yanked on the emergency brake.

Tires screeched on hot pavement, the coupé swerved sharply

to the right, dragged to a screaming stop, at right angles across the thoroughfare. Segurius was thrown forward against the wheel by the sudden stop.

Twenty feet ahead, Jimmy had halted his roadster, was already out of it, running toward the coupé. Segurius threw Diane a vicious glance, raised the revolver once more, sighted on Jimmy's running figure. Diane seized his arm, dragged it backward, and the big revolver exploded into the air.

The slug whined above Jimmy's head, and he covered the short intervening distance in a single leap, pulled open the door of the coupé, reaching for his gun as he did so. Segurius, uttering a roar of rage, shoved Diane back with a thrust of his elbow and leaped out of the car.

His huge bulk struck Jimmy Christopher squarely, and Operator 5 went sprawling backward, to land heavily on the asphalt....

Segurius raised the gun once more, prepared to fire into Jimmy's body. But Jimmy rolled over on the ground twice, so swiftly as to confuse the big man's aim. In that second of breathing space, Operator 5's hand streaked to his shoulder holster, came out with his own automatic. Jimmy's gun spat wickedly at the same moment that Segurius fired. The big man's bullet was a bit wide, and ricocheted off the asphalt, but Operator 5's slug caught Segurius above the heart.

Segurius, for all his size, was smashed backward like a rag doll against the side of the coupé he had just left. Then he sank to the ground, dead.

Men were running toward the scene, and far down the street,

a military patrol came rushing. The city was under martial law, and a uniformed regular army corporal and two privates, were coming on the run.

Jimmy reached out and seized Diane by the arm, dragging her from the coupé and rushing her into the roadster. "Come on," he exclaimed breathlessly. "We've no time for answering questions!"

Diane cast a last look backward at the body of Segurius, slumped against the coupé; then the scene was blotted from her eyes as Jimmy swung the powerful roadster around the corner, speeding east, then south again.

A hail of lead from the rifles of the patrol sang through the air, but they were already around the corner. Jimmy handled the wheel with consummate skill, avoiding the few pedestrians who were hurrying toward the scene, attracted by the shots. Soon they were out of the neighborhood, and Diane breathed a sigh of relief.

She exclaimed, "Jimmy! How did you happen to come back after us?"

Jimmy grinned tightly, keeping his eyes ahead. "Pure accident. I noticed that coupé at the corner as I drove away, and thought it might be following me. So I doubled on my tracks and drove clear around the block. I came back into our street just in time to see him push you into the car. I came after you, and you know the rest."

"Thank God you did," Diane breathed. "That man—was mad, Jimmy. He—he was the man who brought me to the Dragon Master's house."

"I wonder what he wanted with you now," Jimmy asked,

frowning. "It doesn't check up—first they let you go, then they try to grab you again—"

"He—he said that the Master had left the city, but that he had remained behind because"—she blushed a little—"because he loved me! He said he had braved the Dragon Master's anger by staying behind in order to be—near me!"

Jimmy smiled. "He was a very discriminating man, Di. Too bad I had to kill him."

She shuddered. Suddenly her eyes grew calculating. "Are you taking me to the airport, Jimmy?"

He nodded. "There's no time now to drop you off. Captain Loring will be getting impatient, and I want to take off before he phones back to headquarters and learns that General Falk didn't authorize me to use his plane. You can drive this car back home."

Diane settled back in her seat, let her lids cover her eyes. She said nothing, but she had her own ideas about what she was going to do when she reached the airport.

WHEN THEY reached Mitchell Field, they met a scene of bustling activity. A dozen Martin bombers were being warmed up on the line. Behind them on the field, a like number of trim pursuit planes were being checked over by mechanics.

Jimmy frowned when he saw Captain Loring standing with a group of other fliers, grouped about the tall, ramrod figure of Major Crothers. Operator 5 knew Major Crothers well. He was the ranking flight commander in the East, by virtue of seniority, and a martinet of the worst kind.

Loring saw Jimmy and Diane approaching across the field and hurried over, shook hands with both of them. He said to

Jimmy, "I don't know what you had up your sleeve, old man, but Crothers says that General Falk didn't authorize you to go up with me."

"I didn't say that he did," Jimmy told him.

Loring grinned. "I know you didn't."

"Look here, Captain," Jimmy said earnestly, "I've got to get into the occupied territory in New England. I wanted you to land me—"

Loring shook his head. "Sorry, Operator 5. I'd damn well like to take you, but it couldn't be done. As you see, I've been superseded in command here by Crothers, and he's hot against you. Apparently you raised Falk's dander—"

He stopped as Major Crothers approached them, his bushy eyebrows almost meeting in a frown of disapproval.

Crothers glanced from Diane to Jimmy, then said heavily: "Operator 5, I'll have to ask you to leave the field. We're going up in a half hour to attack Wetherill. I understand you wanted Loring here to take you into New England—"

"Yes, sir!" Jimmy broke in eagerly. "I've got a scheme—"

Crothers shook his head. "General Falk particularly instructed me about you. He wants no interference with his plans from you. We are throwing every available man and plane against the enemy's position. The time granted you by Washington has expired, and—" His tone took on a slight tinge of the malicious, "—we are going to try to regain the territory we lost by following your advice. I repeat—I must ask you to leave the field at once!"

"Do you mean to say," Jimmy gasped, "that General Falk is going to send men marching against New England, and expose

114

them to destruction by those rockets? Don't you see, Major, that by massing his forces in this way, the general is inviting anni-hilation?"

"We are no longer asking your advice, Operator 5," Crothers said stiffly. "The handful of desperadoes and criminals compris-ing this Dragon Master's forces will be quickly overwhelmed by the manpower we are launching against them. And now, if you will excuse me—"

He bowed, stood waiting for Jimmy to leave.

Jimmy glanced hotly at Loring, who shrugged helplessly.

Suddenly Operator 5 said, "Sorry to have made a nuisance of myself, Major. I'll go. And I wish you the best of luck!"

He took Diane's arm, led her from the field, under the suspi-cious scrutiny of the major.

"What are you going to do now, Jimmy?" Diane asked him as he tooled the roadster out and away from the field. "Will you give up the idea of getting into Wetherill?"

He laughed shortly. "Give it up? I've got to go more than ever now. Think of all those men marching to death! The Dragon Master won't let them get far—"

He stopped as a shrill whistling sound cut through the air from above.

Tight-lipped, he stepped on the brake, pulled the car up, and craned his head toward the skies. A comet-like object was hurtling through the air at incredible speed, winging downward toward Mitchell Field.

Suddenly it struck, and a blinding, deafening explosion shook the ground with a shock like an earthquake. Waves of sound rolled back to them with shattering impact against their eardrums.

And from Mitchell Field, a tall column of flame seared into the air, while bits of earth and wreckage of planes and hangars were shot upward. Debris rained down upon them for long minutes, while panic-stricken men who had been on the outskirts of the field ran from the scene in blind fear. But the men who had been on the field itself would no longer run.

Diane, white-faced, whispered, "Jimmy! All those men! Captain Loring, Major Crothers—they—they're all—" Her voice broke.

Jimmy Christopher nodded grimly. "Not a plane or a flier left. I wonder how many other fields the Dragon Master is striking at the same time?"

He turned to the wheel, got the car in motion.

"Shouldn't we stay and help in the first-aid, Jimmy—?"

"They're past first-aid, Di. Our job isn't here."

"*Our* job?" Diane exclaimed gladly.

He nodded. "I'm going to go up in my autogyro. It's the only way to get over. And Di—you win. I'm taking you along. When I land, you'll fly her back here. I wouldn't take you, but I can't let the plane be discovered there, or they'd know somebody had landed inside their lines."

Diane's face was suddenly flushed. "I'm glad I'm going, Jimmy." She glanced back down the road, at what had just been a great flying field but was now no more than a heap of smouldering ruins. "I—I want to do something to help—to stop that!"

CHAPTER 10
TIM'S TRIBULATION

NEW ENGLAND lay like a tortured maiden under the hands of an executioner. On the land, no work was done. Farms went untended while the farmers huddled in their dwellings, fearful lest they attract to themselves the unwelcome attentions of the conquering invaders.

In the cities and towns, industry was at a standstill. Factories did not blow their morning whistles; stores remained closed. Men and women kept off the streets, kept their children at home. They peered furtively through curtained windows at the hard-faced men in the strange blue uniforms, who passed outside. And whenever a group of these hammered upon a neighbor's door, they breathed deep sighs of sympathy. For they knew that the errand of those men was one of pillage and torture.

Cries of agony often sounded from the homes that the uniformed men had entered—cries of agony accompanied by loud, brutish laughter and ribald jests.

The invaders, originally few in number, had augmented their strength by throwing open the jails and enlisting in their ranks the felons, the murderers, the enemies of society who had been confined there. These men, newly released from prison, with hatred in their hearts, were given weapons and uniforms, and were given power and authority over the citizens who had put them in jail.

All over New England there was an orgy of killing, of torturing, and of robbing and rapine. Men's blood boiled at the things they heard of, at the things they saw done. Yet they were helpless to resist, for they lacked arms. By the law of the country, they, as peaceful citizens, had always been forbidden to carry or possess arms. Now they pitifully felt the lack of them.

All through that day the invaders consolidated their position, promulgated laws and compelled the newspapers to print them. The territory comprising the states of Maine, New Hampshire, Vermont and Rhode Island were declared to be now under the dominion of the Empire of the Dragon. Notice was given that within forty-eight hours every man in the territory would be required to come to his county seat and swear allegiance to the Dragon Emperor. Money in all banks was confiscated, and an order was issued directing that the inhabitants of each town supply a certain quantity of food and supplies to the armed forces of the invaders. Every civilian passing a uniformed invader in the streets must stand aside and doff his hat, under penalty of instant death.

Within Fort Wetherill, the man with the black hood and gloves sat at the head of a long table. He was speaking to a half-dozen men sitting around the table. At his right was General Komroff, twirling his long mustache. All of these men, except their leader, wore light-blue uniforms and caps similar to the officers' hats in the late Imperial German army. They were the highest ranking officers in the newer imperial army of the Dragon Empire. On the front of each cap was the same figure of the coiled dragon which appeared on the flag that now flew above the turrets of Wetherill—the flag that had displaced the Stars and Stripes.

118

The hooded man seemed to have gained in pomposity, in authority, since he had taken over active charge of his forces. His voice had an edge of steel now, as his sparkling eyes peered out through the slits in the hood at his generals—generals who had, only a short while before, been felons in the penal colony of Guiana.

"We have New England in our grip," he was saying. "The people will bow to our will—and those who don't—" he glanced sideways at Komroff "—you know how to handle them!"

Komroff smiled, his thick, red lips seeming to grow thicker under the mustache. "Three thousand executions today, Master, have taught them how to obey. We will have no more trouble from the people of New England."

THE MASTER nodded. "We are now ready for the next step. We will occupy Massachusetts, Connecticut and New York." He placed a black-gloved finger on a map on the table. "We will advance along the Erie Canal as far as Lake Ontario, then move south to New York City. All forts of any consequence have been destroyed. There will be little resistance."

"I have reports, Master, that at least two divisions of the United States Army are moving against us from New York. They were a little upset when we destroyed their airports this morning, but they are advancing again now. It is almost night. Shall we send them a little souvenir in the shape of a rocket?"

"I think," said the Dragon Emperor, "that we can wait until the morning. You might send a message to that fool of a General Falk. Tell him that if his troops are not withdrawn immediately, we will launch a rocket against Manhattan Island at dawn."

Komroff's eyes gleamed. "Splendid, Master. They will surely retreat rather than have the richest city in the country destroyed!"

"That is all," said the hooded man. "You may go."

The officers arose and backed out of the room. The Master was left alone. He sat for a while in silence, drumming on the table top. The *tap, tap, tap* of his gloved fingers sounded ominous, funereal.

Abruptly, he pushed back his chair, got up. He made his way out of the room through a small door behind his chair, passed down a small corridor and tried the door of another room. It opened under his touch, and he entered quietly.

This was a bedroom, perhaps one used formerly by the commanding officer of Fort Wetherill. There was no light in the room, and the deepening dusk outside formed weird shadows outside the large double window.

Zara had been lying on the double bed in the center of the room. She sprang up at the sound of the opening door, stood erect facing the Master. She wore a long black dress, molded to her supple figure. It was wrinkled now, and her hair was a bit disarranged from lying on the bed. Her face was drawn and haggard as she put a hand to her breast, waiting for the man to speak.

For a while he said nothing, but stood looking at her. Finally he said: "You are very beautiful, Zara. Even when you do not look your best, you are very beautiful."

She lowered her eyes. Her breasts were rising and falling in fast, uneven rhythm.

The Master went on imperturbably, as if he had not noticed the strain under which she seemed to be laboring.

"That boy, Tim Donovan," he said. "He is very stubborn. Come. We will go and see him again."

She took an impulsive step forward. "Why must you torture the poor lad so? He is so young—"

"Let him speak, then," the hooded man said coldly. "I planned to eliminate Operator 5 by giving a bomb to that girl. She thought it was an instrument for sending a radio beam. In reality, it was a bomb that would have exploded the moment it was plugged into a socket and the key depressed. I thought that she would show it to Operator 5, and that he would try it. But he was too clever. My reports show that he was alive this afternoon."

HE PAUSED, walked up and down the room impatiently. Then he broke out irritably: "Zara, I fear that Operator 5. He is the only one who is not a fool. He must be killed. I must learn from the boy where he lives, where he can be reached. I still have many disciples in New York—disciples who will obey me to the letter. Once I know where Operator 5 can be found—"

"But the boy won't tell you. He is so devoted to—"

"Bah!" the Master's voice broke spitefully. "He can't hold out forever. Come. We will talk to him!"

She drew back. "Must I witness his agony?"

"I said—come!" He spoke softly, but Zara shuddered, and obeyed....

He led the way out into the corridor once more, and down a flight of stairs. There were cells here where prisoners were kept. They were all empty except one.

The hooded man motioned to a uniformed guard, who opened the cell before which they stood. It was in total darkness until the guard pressed a switch which brought to life a small electric bulb in the ceiling.

Zara, who stood behind the hooded man, uttered a gasp at the sight of Tim Donovan, spread-eagled against the wall facing the door.

Tim's wrists had been tied to two staples in the wall. The staples were so high up that the lad's feet barely touched the floor. He had been stripped to the waist, and the muscles of his shoulders showed in bulges where the strain of his weight fell. Across his chest and stomach there were raw welts, and on the floor at his feet lay the long, snaky whip which had inflicted them.

Tim's head was bowed, resting on his chest. He looked up when the light went on and glared at the hooded man. His face was streaked with sweat, and his parched lips hung open.

The hooded man said genially: "How do you feel, my boy?"

Tim tried to talk, but his voice cracked in his dry throat. He gulped, wet his lips with his tongue, and croaked, "Go to hell, Mr. Bogey-man!"

The hooded man clucked deprecatingly, shrugged and glanced at Zara.

"You see, my dear, how obstinate he is?" He turned to the boy, and his geniality was gone. "Are you ready to talk? Where does Operator 5 live? Speak quickly!"

Tim glanced at Zara, saw the look of compassion in her eyes, and essayed a weak smile. Then his gaze hardened as it swung to the Master. "You won't have to find Operator 5, Mr. Bogey-man," he said hoarsely. "He'll come here after you pretty soon!"

The Master stepped close to Tim.

"Boy," he said ominously, "you will talk—soon. If you are wise, you will talk now. It is better to talk than to suffer." Slowly he bent and picked up the heavy whip, cracked it through the air. The whip was perhaps four feet long, with a hard, leather handle, and it made a terrifying *cracking* sound through the air.

Tim's muscles involuntarily contracted at the snap of the whip. He had felt that lash on his body already. It had sent excruciating agony through every fiber of his body, had left him weak, faint, throbbing with pain that had not left him yet. Now he must endure more.

He clamped his mouth hard shut, and waited, hanging there by his wrists.

The Master snarled, "All right. Have it your way!"

He stepped back, swung the whip high. It swished through the air, snapped with a sickening, crackling thud across Tim Donovan's body.

The boy stiffened as the lash raked across him, and an unquenchable cry of pain was torn from his lips. A great, red welt appeared where the whip had struck. He bit his lip to keep back the choked cry of agony that welled in his throat, kept his eyes fixed on the hooded man.

Once more the Master raised the whip. Once more he brought it down—again and again….

Standing behind him, Zara closed her eyes to shut out the

sight of Tim's young, agonized face. But she could not shut out the sound of the lash as it *slapped* into the boy's body....

CHAPTER 11
OVER THE ENEMY LINES

A TRIM autogyro hovered over the coast of Rhode Island, moving leisurely through the gathering night. The two figures in the cockpit were carefully scanning the terrain below. To the east, the dark expanse of the Atlantic stretched out into the mysterious night. To the north, there was visible the town of Newport, with its cluster of small buildings. Within an area of five miles of the town there could also be seen several huge mounds of debris, still smoldering. They were the ruins of the forts, formerly clustered at this spot, which had been destroyed by rockets. One structure still stood, and from its turret there was flaunted the black flag of the Dragon Empire. This was Fort Wetherill.

One of the figures in the autogyro raised a hand, pointed down toward a small patch of ground perhaps a mile from the fort. The plane moved toward that place, then descended gracefully, slowly.

As it touched the ground, its two occupants legged from the cockpit. Jimmy Christopher helped Diane out, and then they examined their surroundings. A road ran eastward toward Fort Wetherill not a hundred feet from where they stood. Beyond the road there was an old farmhouse, apparently untenanted.

Jimmy Christopher smiled at Diane, said, "All right, Di. Now, get in the plane and take her away. I'll work along toward the fort—"

He stopped as Diane shook her head stubbornly. "No, Jimmy. I'm not going back. If this is to be your last adventure, it's going to be mine, too!"

Operator 5 exclaimed impatiently, "But, Di, I told you that you'd have to go back—"

"But I didn't say I would—and I won't! You'll just have to make the best of it. So there!"

Jimmy glared at her. "Di, you've got to go back. I won't have you risking your life—"

"All right then, I'll go back—if you will! Who gave you the monopoly of risking your life?" She suddenly took an impulsive step closer to him. "Don't you see, Jimmy?" she went on almost pleadingly. "I want to share this with you. I want to help. I know what you're going to do. You're going to try to get into one of those rockets somehow and direct it back against Wetherill. You're going to throw your life away deliberately for the sake of destroying the fort and the rocket contraption. And, Jimmy—I couldn't bear to fly back to New York alone, knowing what you're going to do. Jimmy—" her voice dropped almost to a whisper "—let me die with you!"

Whatever he might have said to her mad plea remained unsaid, for just then, from the direction of the road, came voices, shouts, the sound of running feet. Jimmy seized Diane's arm and dragged her back into the shadows. "They must have seen us land!" he whispered. "They'll scour the countryside for us!"

The shouting voices resolved into figures of uniformed men,

who, when they saw the autogyro, came running toward it with rifles raised.

Jimmy dragged Di backward, farther into the protection of the shadows. There were half a dozen of the uniformed men, and while they closed in on the plane, Jimmy and Diane stole back toward the road.

Suddenly Jimmy dropped to the ground, dragged Diane down with him. He had acted none too soon. The powerful headlamps of a car swung around a curve in the road from the direction of the fort. Brakes squealed, the car halted at the edge of the road, opposite the plane, and not ten feet from where Jimmy and Diane crouched!

An officer with a thick, bestial face descended, and called to the men around the plane. He spoke in French, and Jimmy assumed that these were a contingent of the escaped felons from Guiana. "Where is he? Have you captured him?"

"No," one of the men shouted in reply. "No one is here. The plane is empty."

"Then," the commander called out testily, still in French, which both Jimmy and Diane understood, "whoever came in it cannot be far away. It must be a spy. Spread out. Be careful. Shoot on sight. *But do not let him escape you!*" He turned, put a foot on the running board. "I will return to the fort and send out others to help you. There will be a nice reward for the man who is first to find this spy!"

THE OFFICER stepped up on the running board, and Jimmy Christopher leaped from the shadows, automatic in his hand. The ugly commander half-turned, startled, but Jimmy's gun was boring into the small of his back. "Make no sound!" Jimmy warned. "Get into the car quietly."

The officer stood rigid, and the chauffeur turned his head, saw Jimmy, and opened his mouth to shout. But he never uttered a sound. For at the window behind him appeared the flushed face of Diane. She had run around the car from behind, and had drawn out the small nickel-plated pistol she always carried in her handbag. She was pressing it against the back of the chauffeur's neck. He needed no further warning to be silent. The cry died on his lips.

Jimmy prodded the officer into the rear of the car and said, "Sit down—and keep your hands clasped in your lap."

The officer's thick lips twisted into a smile. "You are bold," he said in French. "But you dare not shoot. My men would hear and be upon you in a moment—"

"That's right," Jimmy agreed. "But I can do this." He holstered the automatic, and the officer's eyes narrowed as he saw his captor unarmed. His hand went swiftly to the holster at his belt. But Jimmy's right fist came up in a flashing arc, catching him on the point of the chin with a nasty crack.

The officer's head was jerked backward, cracked against the window, and the man slumped in his seat. Jimmy unceremoniously pushed his unconscious body to the floor, then said to Diane: "Good work, Di. Now get in. I've got the driver covered."

He had his automatic out again, and the muzzle was pointing at the chauffeur. Diane opened the door on the far side from the searchers around the autogyro, stepped into the car.

"Now, my friend," Jimmy said to the driver, "turn around and take us back to the fort."

The chauffeur stared into the muzzle of the gun, terrified. *"Je ne comprends pas!"* he muttered.

Jimmy repeated the order in French, and the driver reluctantly swung the car in a U-turn, headed back toward Wetherill. Behind them, the searchers were fanning out, covering every inch of ground, poking their flashlights into every shadow.

Diane asked breathlessly, "What's next, Jimmy?"

"Whatever is next," he told her, "is in the laps of the gods." He held his automatic so that the chauffeur could see it in the rear-vision mirror.

"You will drive to the fort, my friend, and enter through the gate," he commanded in French. "In case you should have any ideas of warning the guard at the gate, I can assure you that the next words you speak after that will be uttered in hell. Understand?"

"Yes, yes, monsieur, I understand!" The driver gulped.

In another minute or so, the headlights picked up the bulk of Fort Wetherill, just off the road. The driver swung the car to the left, pulling up just before the gate. A guard, who apparently knew the chauffeur, waved to him, and he drove through the ironwork barrier.

In the courtyard, many men were hurrying about under bright incandescents. Mechanics were working feverishly on half a dozen armored cars, mounting machine guns at the loopholes. These armored cars had been commandeered by the invaders.

The driver parked the car in a far corner of the courtyard,

under the wall of the fort, obeying Jimmy's instructions. No one paid any attention. A guard detail passed them right by without glancing at the car.

The chauffeur half-turned in his seat, started to speak. Jimmy said in English, "Sorry about this, old man," and brought the butt of his automatic down on the man's head. The chauffeur collapsed in the seat and slid under the wheel.

"Now," Jimmy Christopher said to Diane, "all we have to do is get into the fort!"

TIM DONOVAN hadn't talked under the lash. But the lad's drooping body, still hanging from his wrists in the cell, showed what a price he had paid for his stubbornness.

The strain on Tim's muscles was unbearable, and he constantly kept stretching his toes toward the floor in an effort to take some of the pull from his shoulders and arms. Beads of sweat trickled down Tim's chest. Great livid welts looked raw in the light and his breathing was choked with pain.

His head was bowed on his chest, and he was biting his lip. He knew he couldn't hold out much longer....

He was alone now, for the guard had departed after the last visit of the Master. They had left him alone with his misery. "It will be a little while before I return again," the Master had chuckled. "Perhaps, by then, you will be begging for a chance to talk!"

Now Tim's head jerked up as he heard footsteps on the stone flagging outside the cell. For a second, he thought it must be the Master, returning to resume his cruel sport with the whip.

Then he realized that the steps were too light to be those of the Master.

His red-rimmed eyes fixed themselves on the grating of the cell door. They lighted up as they saw the figure of the beautiful woman whose name he did not know, but in whose glance he had seen compassion earlier that night when she watched the master ply the whip.

The woman hesitated a moment outside the door. Then she swiftly inserted a key in the lock, pulled open the door, and stepped inside.

In her hand there was a knife which gleamed under the single electric light bulb in the ceiling. Tim's eyes opened wide, settled on the knife.

The woman came close, said with deep-throated sympathy, "You poor lad!"

She reached up swiftly, slashed at the ropes which bound his wrists to the wall. The sudden slackening of the strain against his arm and shoulder muscles sent twinges of fire coursing through Tim's body. He found himself too weak to stand. His legs buckled, and he slumped in a heap on the floor. Tingling needle shocks prickled at his arms and legs. He tried to get up, failed....

Zara's white hands raised him. "You must walk," she whispered urgently. "I am going to take you out of here—to help you get away. I—I can't let that fiend kill you by inches. Come!"

She helped him walk through the cell door. Tim gazed at her gratefully. "You're taking an awful chance, lady," he croaked. "That guy'll skin you alive if he finds out you helped me."

"I don't care!" she exclaimed defiantly. "I—I can't stand it any longer."

As he walked, Tim's strength came back to him. He began to feel hungry. He had not eaten for twenty-four hours.

Zara led him, not to the staircase by which she had come down, but to a rear exit which took them up a flight of rickety stairs and out into a courtyard. Though the courtyard was well lit, they were in deep shadow.

Zara whispered to him: "I'm going to help you get through the gate. We'll work along the wall behind the cars, and I'll go ahead. I'll send the guard on an errand, and then you'll sneak out. Stay off the road, but go parallel to it until you reach an old farmhouse. You can't miss it; it's the first building you'll come to. Nobody lives there, and nobody bothers about the place. You can hide there. From then on, may God protect you!"

"Gee, lady," Tim said, his voice thickening, "I hate to go and leave you here. That Mr. Bogey-man—"

THE WORDS died on his lips as he heard a stirring in the shadow of the nearest car. A dark shape took form beside him, and his blood froze. Zara uttered a gasp of dismay.

Tim's chin jutted, his fists clenched. He wouldn't be taken again. He was only sorry that the beautiful lady had got herself mixed up with him. It would go hard with her.

His eyes strained through the gloom toward the shadow. And suddenly the shadowy figure sprang forward, uttering a muffled, joyful cry: "Tim!"

Tim's heart seemed to turn a somersault into his throat.

Tears of relief flooded his eyes. "Jimmy!" he whispered hoarsely. "Jimmy! I knew you'd come! This lady got me out—"

And he stopped right there. Exhaustion, pain, weariness and shock claimed him. He collapsed into Jimmy Christopher's arms in a dead faint….

Operator 5 raised the boy's frail, tortured body in his arms tenderly. Even in the dark, he could discern the raw, red welts, and he cursed softly under his breath.

Zara had started to back away at the first intimation of an alien presence there, but Jimmy saw her and called out, very low, "Wait, please!"

She stopped, half fearful, uncertain.

Jimmy carried Tim into the car, where Diane was sitting, and she moved over so that he could stretch the lad out full-length on the seat. Then she took Tim's head on her lap, caressed his wet, matted hair. Her fingers touched the horrid wounds on his chest, and a low moan escaped her.

Jimmy Christopher stepped to Zara, who watched him dully, with questioning eyes. He asked, "You helped Tim to—escape from in there?"

She nodded.

"I can never repay you." In the dark, his eyes studied her white face, and he went on: "I don't know who you are, or what your position is here. But if there is anything I can do to help you—"

She said softly, "I can see now how you inspire such loyalty. I can see why that boy was willing to be tortured even to death rather than say one word that might harm you. You give loyalty for loyalty, do you not, Operator 5?"

She glanced worriedly toward the main entrance of the building, where many men in uniform were passing in and out. "You must go quickly. If you came to save the boy, you have him there. Make your escape. You were clever enough to get in; you will be clever enough to get out. But for God's sake do not remain here. At any moment you may be discovered—"

"I came to do more than save Tim," Jimmy Christopher told Zara quietly. "I came to destroy your Dragon Emperor." He watched her keenly. "And I think you will help me!"

She stared at him. "You are mad! What can you do—one man, alone? He is surrounded by guards, well protected—"

Jimmy put a hard hand on her soft white arm. "You are no friend of the Dragon Emperor. You, too, want to see him destroyed. Am I right?"

A SIBILANT sigh escaped her lips. "If I only could! I am Zara. I am she whom the Dragon Emperor plans to make his empress. Yet I am a prisoner. Should I attempt to escape, he would leave no corner of the earth unturned until he found me—and his punishment would be far worse than death. That is why I dared not go with the boy just now, but sent him on his way alone. If only I could be free!"

There was such a depth of feeling in her voice—such fierce hatred—that Jimmy was impressed. "I can help you," he told her. "Do you know how the rocket catapult is operated?"

She nodded, gazing at him queerly. "Yes. The rockets are equipped with stabilizers and ailerons. A man sits inside it and guides it to its destination. When it strikes, the man perishes. The Dragon Emperor has a group of dupes, whom he has hypnotized by his magic oratory. They are ready to die, thinking that by destroying the instruments of war, and sacrificing their lives, they will bring to this earth the peace and good will toward men that Christ preached, and for which He, too, died. They—"

"I know that," Jimmy broke in. "I want to know about the rockets. How are they released?"

"The catapult is operated by a lever in a room on the main floor. The whole machinery was brought over from the ship on which it was originally used. I do not know the principle, but I know that by throwing the lever, the rocket is released."

"Tell me," Jimmy asked her, "could you pull that lever?"

"I could. But why—"

"And could you get me to the rocket without our being observed?"

"Yes. There is a rear stairway that is not being used now. But what good would it do—?"

"We could arrange," Jimmy told her calmly, "for you to pull that lever at a certain time. I would be in the rocket when it is released. And I would guide the rocket back against this place. Do you understand?"

She gasped. "You would throw away your life?"

"Why not? I am one man. Millions have died for less worthy purposes. Will you take me to the rocket?"

She hesitated. "Operator 5," she said, "you are a very brave man."

But Jimmy pressed his questions. "Is this the only catapult the Dragon Emperor has?"

"Yes. He had another on a ship off the Florida coast, but

that ship was wrecked last night on the reefs near the Bahama Islands. This is the only catapult he has now."

"All right," Jimmy said. "Wait here a moment."

He hurried back to the car. Tim was conscious again, and he smiled weakly at Jimmy.

"How are you, kid?" Operator 5 asked with an affectation of roughness. "I can see you can take it!"

Tim grinned. "I kept thinking of you all the time, Jimmy. I knew you'd keep mum, so I had to do the same."

Jimmy glanced at Diane. "Look, Di," he said. "I'm giving you orders now, and I want them obeyed without argument."

He went on swiftly, in a matter-of-fact voice: "I'm going back into the fort with Zara. You'll wait here, in the car, Tim in back, and you behind the wheel. In a few minutes, Zara will come out. As soon as she gets in the car, *you drive like hell!* The gate is open. Go right through—ride the guard down if you have to—and put as much space between this place and yourselves as possible. Is that clear?"

Tim asked innocently, "But where will you be, Jimmy?"

Operator 5 averted his eyes, answered evasively: "I'll—come in another car—right after you." He avoided Tim's gaze, looked at Diane. "You understand, Di?"

SHE WAS breathing hard, and there was unnaturally bright color in her face. "I—understand, Jimmy. But—"

"But nothing!" he broke in harshly. "Those are orders, Di!"

He turned away abruptly, made for the dark shadow against the wall which was Zara.

Diane uttered a little choked cry, scrambled out of the car, murmuring, "Wait a minute Tim, I'll be right back," and ran after Jimmy Christopher. "Jimmy!" she called in a suddenly broken voice. "Jimmy!"

Operator 5 stopped, turned slowly. While Zara watched, Diane ran up to him, stopped short within a foot, her hands at her sides.

"Jimmy!" she said huskily. "Are you—going away—without even saying—goodbye?"

His face in the dark was inscrutable, but she could almost feel the tenseness of him. "You're going to your death, Jimmy. I—!" She couldn't say any more.

Jimmy Christopher, grim-faced, took her in his arms. Her soft, warm body quivered under his touch. "Diane, darling," he whispered into her ear, "it would have been easier to do without the goodbye." He crushed her to him. "Tell Dad—goodbye for me!" And then, with a quick, abrupt motion he released her, pushed her way. She swayed slightly, but he turned away and said gruffly to Zara: "Let's go!"

Zara opened her mouth to say something, but at the glance in his eye she left it unsaid, turned and silently led the way back through the doorway from which she had led Tim a few moments before.

In the courtyard, Diane put out a hand to support herself against the wall, keeping her eyes on the figures of Zara and Jimmy until they disappeared and the door closed behind them. Jimmy did not look back. She had known he wouldn't. There was a heaviness in her heart that she knew would be with her as long as she lived. She longed to go after him, but the thought of Tim, wounded and weak in the car, checked her.

The boy raised himself up on the seat, called out softly, "Di! You better come back here and get in. You have to be ready to drive away."

"Coming, Tim." She tried to make her voice sound natural. She couldn't tell the boy now. Later, she wouldn't have to. He would know.

She moved as if with leaden feet, got into the car behind the wheel. Tim was curiously examining a small black box. It had a socket at one end, and a key at the top.

She exclaimed, "Be careful with that, Tim!"

"What is it, Di?" he asked.

"It's a bomb. Jimmy must have left it here. He thinks it's set to explode when you plug it into an outlet and depress the key."

"You don't say so," Tim observed. "A bomb, huh?"

She watched his fresh young interest in the dangerous box. She tried to make conversation, so that he wouldn't notice her unnatural quietness. "It's supposed to be a very powerful explosive. Jimmy thinks there's enough in that box to blow up a whole city block."

"That's interesting," Tim said, half to himself. "Say, I've got an idea. Let's see what we can work out with this thing."

Grimacing with pain, he got to his knees on the floor of the car....

DIANE PAID no attention to him. Her mind was awhirl. She could not make herself accept the fact that Jimmy Christopher was, at that very moment, probably, preparing to step into the rocket lying in the catapult which was projecting from the top of the wall directly above her. She could not bring herself to realize that he was going to shoot himself into space, and then to bring that rocket right back to this spot—to destroy the fort and himself.

Minutes elapsed and her restless nervousness grew greater and greater, while Tim stooped at her feet.

Suddenly Diane's eyes started with terror. Two men were coming toward their car. They wore the uniforms of officers, and they hurried, as if they were bent upon an errand. She could not tell whether they were making for the car she and Tim were in, or for one of the others in the row. If these were reserve autos for the officers' use, it was probable that they would pick the first in the row—which was this one!

Breathless, she watched them until they were within a dozen feet of the car. Then she was sure they were going to get into this one. Swiftly, she made up her mind. Tim was hurt, weak. If he were caught again, he could not survive further torture. As for herself, she didn't care to live any longer.

She stooped swiftly, whispering, "Tim, you'll have to drive the car. I'm going out. Remember, one of us has to be here!"

Before the bewildered Tim could comprehend what she meant, she had opened the door, stepped out into the courtyard, and slammed the door behind her.

The two officers stopped, astounded. Then one of them swore softly. They started toward her, but she ran forward to keep them from coming too close to the car and discovering that there was another person in it. She recognized one of them. He was a man who had been present at the brownstone house in New York when she had been a prisoner of the Master. He was a small, wizened man, and she remembered that he had been called Leon. He had been one of those who had turned her loose with the bomb.

Leon recognized her at once, and a thin smile spread on his lips. He sprang forward, seized her by the arm.

"So," he said. "This will indeed be a surprise for the Master!" He turned, dragging her with him toward the main entrance. She offered no resistance, glad to get as far away from the car as possible. The other officer with Leon protested:

"But wait! Who is this?"

"This," Leon snarled, "is one whom the Master will welcome. If she is here, it means that Operator 5 is near!"

The other officer followed, still protesting. "But we were going to investigate that autogyro that was sighted. Why—?"

"That can wait!" Leon snapped. "She must have come in that autogyro—with Operator 5. The Master will want to give her a little pleasure ride—in a rocket!"

Behind them, Tim gazed after them, his eyes narrowed. He understood now what Diane had meant. She had deliberately given herself up to save him. His mind worked swiftly, trying to devise a means of rescuing her....

CHAPTER 12
THE FIGHT ON THE PARAPET

J IMMY CHRISTOPHER had left Diane standing there, leaning against the wall, and had followed Zara into the building. He knew that Diane would be watching for him to turn and throw her a last farewell gesture, but he dared not do it, lest she race after him, try to stop him again.

Inside, once the door had closed behind them, Zara led him swiftly down a flight of stairs into the section of the fort where Tim had been confined. They even passed the cell where he had been strung up, but she refrained from pointing it out to him. At the rear of the fort, she led him up another flight of stairs, past the first and second landings. There was no one about, and she explained over her shoulder:

"We haven't been using this portion of the building. The Master has made his quarters in the assembly hall downstairs, and he quarters very few of his officers in this building. You see, he doesn't trust them all."

Jimmy followed her, making no comment. As they turned into the third-floor landing, Zara, who was in the lead, uttered a low exclamation and stepped hastily back.

But a harsh voice called to her: "Ah! The beautiful Zara! What do you find of interest in this part of the fort?" Jimmy, who was below her on the landing, was invisible to the speaker as yet.

Zara stiffened, stepped up onto the landing. Jimmy drew his automatic, crouched grim-faced behind her, a couple of steps down. He hoped that he would remain undiscovered by whoever

140

it was that had spoken. A gunshot here might bring dozens of men from other parts of the building down on them, making it impossible for him to carry out his plan.

Zara was saying, "I am merely inspecting the place, General Komroff. A very interesting thing, a fort."

The man who faced her was the Dragon Emperor's right-hand man, Komroff. He came closer to her, his small, pig-like eyes traveling up and down her supple figure in lascivious admiration.

"I have been longing, Zara, for a chance to talk to you alone."

"Yes," she countered. She knew very well what he wanted. She had seen the way he constantly looked at her, even when the emperor was present. A woman is never blind to such attention, even though it may be extremely unwelcome to her. She put up a hand as he came close to her, his eyes gleaming.

"I have wanted to tell you, Zara, that I have never thought about another woman the way I think about you. You are beautiful. Too beautiful for that man in the leather mask!"

His hairy hand came up to her shoulder, stroked it. "Say the word, Zara, and you and I will take away his empire from him. I command the army, and they will obey me. We can go on to conquer the world together."

He must have seen the loathing in her eyes, for he suddenly snarled:

"So! I am not good enough for you! We shall see if you are a woman who can resist Ladislav Komroff!" His arms went around her in a bear crush that choked the breath from her body. "After I am through with you—"

Operator 5 blazed death at the uniformed men nearest the rocket!

He stopped as Jimmy Christopher leaped up the steps toward them. Komroff swore madly in a foreign tongue. He pushed Zara away from him, his hand going to his side holster. Zara went staggering backward, and Jimmy leaped in, diving for the gun hand of Komroff. He wanted no shooting, nothing to attract others.

Komroff jerked his hand out of the holster, and the revolver went clattering on the floor. Jimmy came in at him, both fists pistoning, smashing blow after blow at the big man's face....
KOMROFF'S NOSE suddenly spurted red, and he uttered a great shout of rage, springing in with both arms spread wide to crush Jimmy Christopher.

Jimmy sidestepped him and sent two swift jabs to Komroff's jaw. Out of the corner of his eye, he saw the woman picking up the big man's revolver, and he cried:

"No shooting, Zara!"

In that instant, Komroff was on him again, his huge arms encircling Jimmy's slim waist. Jimmy ducked, trying to evade the grip, but the two massive arms closed about him, squeezing the breath from him.

Komroff's face was close to his now, and the other's foul breath suffused his nostrils. Jimmy tried to break the hold by jabbing out with both elbows, but Komroff only laughed, pressed tighter, lifted him off the floor. Jimmy hung in the big man's punishing grip, and Komroff started to run toward the wall.

Jimmy knew what that meant. Komroff would release him at the last second and his body would be smashed against the wall, with the added weight of Komroff's body to crush him.

Jimmy had seen that thing done often in the Balkans, where men fought with their fists, their shoes, their teeth—with anything that nature or the devil had equipped them with. And he had seen the broken bodies of men after they had been rushed against the wall. There was only one defense against this attack, and he used it.

Before Komroff had taken three steps, Jimmy pulled his head back as far as it would go, then brought it forward hard. The top of his skull struck with a sickening thud against Komroff's jaw, and the big man's rush was broken in mid-stride. His grip on Jimmy relaxed, and he slid to the floor, slack-eyed, with a broken jaw.

Jimmy's head was spinning from the blow as he scrambled to his feet. Zara was gazing at him wide-eyed. He swayed for a moment on his feet, looked down at the big body at his feet. And curiously enough at this moment, when he was on the way to give up his life, the huge Komroff, lying there inert, brought to his mind a line of poetry that he had often recited by heart as a boy:

> And the great lord of Luna
>> Fell at that deadly stroke,
> As falls on Mount Avernus
>> A thunder-smitten oak.

It was from the Lays of Ancient Rome. And the sight of Komroff toppling to the floor had brought it back to him vividly. He closed his eyes to shut out the dizziness, then opened them in a second and said to Zara: "Let's go!"

She was standing there with shining eyes, holding the gun she had picked up from the floor. She said:

"Operator 5, it is not right that a man like you should give up his life. You are so brave, so strong; and the girl whom you left below—"

"Let's go!" he repeated, his voice grating with harshness.

She shrugged. "You are a strange man," she murmured, "who fights his way toward—death!" Then she turned, led the way rapidly to the top floor. They stopped before a low window that led out to a balcony. "If you follow the balcony around the bend," she told him, "you will find the catapult. There is no use in my taking you there, for I do not understand how it works anyway. I only know that you strap yourself in the cockpit, and cover it up. There is a handle inside to guide it by."

Jimmy nodded. "I'll know how to work it. You go down to the lever. In just five minutes"—he glanced at his wrist watch, compared it with hers—"you will pull the lever. I will be in the rocket."

Her eyes rested on him a second. "I hope, Operator 5," she said, "that we will meet again—in some other, better world!"

Then she turned and was gone....

JIMMY CHRISTOPHER stepped through the window, then made his way around the parapet. As he turned the corner, he stopped short, staring in amazement. There were a dozen men here, in uniform. Behind them, far to one corner, stood a man who wore a leather mask and leather gloves. He was speaking in a voice filled with hate, and he was saying: "My dear young lady, when you land in New York City, you will see it for the last time. In the split second before the explosion, you will hardly have time to think of whether your friend Operator 5 is still alive or dead. And after that second, it will make no difference."

Jimmy glanced toward the edge of the parapet, and his blood ran cold. There, set into freshly cemented masonry, was a huge steel contraption, with a giant ramrod, and a set of rails upon which rested a large rocket. The rocket was big enough to accommodate a load of explosive as well as one man. But this was no man who sat in the rocket now. It was Diane!

Her wrists were tied to the sides of the rocket, and she was seated facing forward so that she could not see the hooded man behind her. Her face was set.

The hooded man went on: "For the last time, young lady, I ask you—where is Operator 5?"

She threw back over her shoulder, "I don't know!"

The hooded man sighed. "That's too bad!" He motioned to Leon, who stood beside him. "Go down, Leon, to the lever room, and pull the lever. Be sure the guiding handle is set for the proper angle, so that the rocket reaches New York."

Leon bowed. "The handle is set, Master." He started for the corner of the parapet where Jimmy crouched.

And Jimmy leaped into action!

His automatic sprang into his hand, blazed at the uniformed men nearest the rocket. They dropped at the two well-placed slugs, and Jimmy leaped toward the rocket, slipping his jackknife out of his pocket. In his mind were his instructions to Zara—*in five minutes that lever*—!

He pressed the button of the knife, and the blade sprang

open, flashing in the air as he slashed down at the cords that tied Diane's wrists. She looked up at him, cried, "Jimmy! You—!"

Her words were drowned by the bark of Jimmy's automatic as the uniformed men, now recovering from their surprise, rushed toward him. He dropped two, still slashing at the ropes. The others stopped short in their headlong rush, and the hooded man screamed in rage.

Jimmy's knife described another last slashing arc, and the last bond fell away from Diane's wrists. Jimmy stepped away from the rocket, shouting, "Out, Di, quick!" At the same time, he swung his automatic toward the uniformed men, seeking a good shot at the Master. But the hooded man was protected behind a wall of guards. Jimmy, his lips pressed tight together, fired into the thick of them, holding his finger down on the gun until the clip was empty. Diane was out of the rocket.

Suddenly there was a rumbling sound, and the ramrod plunged forward. Jimmy jumped away just in time as the rocket shot along the rails and high up into the air with a series of loud explosions at its tail. The ramrod had set off, within the tail of the rocket, the charges of explosive which propelled it forward.

Jimmy had no time to observe it, for the crowd of uniformed men was upon him once more. He understood now why they hadn't fired at him in return: right behind him, close to the parapet, was a row of rockets similar to the one that had just been sent hurtling through the air. A slug burying itself in one of those would have sent the place to Kingdom Come!

JIMMY HAD no more cartridges in his clip. He backed swiftly toward the window, pushing Diane behind him. His fists pistoned in and out with the precision of a trained fighting machine, and men went down at each blow. He glanced behind, saw that Diane was through the window. He jumped through after her, seized her hand and raced.

Shots followed them, but they were around the turn and down a flight before the first of the pursuers reached the head of the stairs. They raced down the remaining two flights, saw Zara standing in the corridor, bewildered, looking up for the source of the firing.

Jimmy called to her, pushed Diane out the door into the courtyard, waited until Zara was out, then slammed the door.

He raced toward the first car, behind the two women. Diane was piling into the auto, when she stopped and exclaimed:

"Tim! Where's Tim?"

For answer, a head appeared in the second car in the row. "Here!" Tim called. "Don't take that car! This one's ready!" The Irish boy was behind the wheel and already had the car in motion. The doors were swinging open, and Zara and Diane leaped into the rear, Jimmy in front beside Tim. As soon as the doors were closed, Tim gunned the motor, raced toward the gate.

Men appeared at the door through which they had come. Guns roared and the glass was shattered. But Tim tooled the car straight for the gate and shot through.

He turned, grinned at Operator 5. "How's that for a getaway, Jimmy?"

Jimmy Christopher did not smile. "All right, Tim, but it means failure. Wetherill still stands. The rocket contraption is still there, and the hooded man is still alive."

For some reason, Tim Donovan didn't seem to feel bad about it. "I wouldn't worry, Jimmy. The Dragon Emperor'll go far—but in the wrong direction."

Jimmy glanced at the boy. "What—?"

His words were drowned by the shock of the explosion that suddenly rocked the earth under them. A holocaust seemed to have struck at them. It was as if a sheet of fire had come down and struck the earth. The car swerved, and Tim fought the wheel, kept it straight in the road.

They all looked back, and a slow smile appeared on Jimmy's lips. Of Fort Wetherill, there was no sign whatever! The fort, with its rockets from hell, had been wiped from the face of the earth!

Diane exclaimed, "W-what happened?"

Tim Donovan laughed infectiously. "I found out that Jimmy was right about that box, Di. It really was explosive."

"What do you mean, Tim?"

The boy explained. "That box bomb you left in the car, Jimmy. While we were waiting for you, I wired it up to the battery, and connected the key on it to the starter. When they came out after us they naturally got in the first car in the row, and stepped on the starter. Well, I guess it was a bomb!"

Jimmy Christopher started to laugh, glancing back at Zara and Diane.

"Tim," he said, "the next time I want to give up my life for my country, I'll ask you about it first."

"What do you mean by that, Jimmy?"

Jimmy Christopher looked back, exchanged a meaningful

150

glance with Diane. "Oh, nothing, Tim," he said. "Skip it. It was just an idle remark!"